THE HIGHLY EFFECTIVE DETECTIVE

Goes to the Dogs

ALSO BY RICHARD YANCEY

ADULT FICTION

The Highly Effective Detective
A Burning in Homeland

MEMOIR

Confessions of a Tax Collector

CHILDREN'S FICTION

The Extraordinary Adventures of Alfred Kropp
Alfred Kropp: The Seal of Solomon

THE HIGHLY EFFECTIVE DETECTIVE
Goes to the Dogs

RICHARD YANCEY

Thomas Dunne Books
St. Martin's Minotaur
New York

THOMAS DUNNE BOOKS.
An imprint of St. Martin's Press.

THE HIGHLY EFFECTIVE DETECTIVE GOES TO THE DOGS. Copyright © 2008 by Richard Yancey. All rights reserved. Printed in the United States of America. For information, address St. Martin's Press, 175 Fifth Avenue, New York, N.Y. 10010.

www.thomasdunnebooks.com
www.minotaurbooks.com

Library of Congress Cataloging-in-Publication Data

Yancey, Richard.
  The highly effective detective goes to the dogs / Richard Yancey.—1st ed.
      p. cm.
  ISBN-13: 978-0-312-34753-6
  ISBN-10: 0-312-34753-7
  1. Private investigators—Fiction. 2. Dogs—Fiction. I. Title.
  PS3625.A675H55 2008
813'.6—dc22

2008018098

First Edition: August 2008

10 9 8 7 6 5 4 3 2 1

To Sandy, with love

NOVEMBER 7

ONE

I was sitting at my desk, staring out the window into the drizzly gray light falling behind the Ely Building, when Felicia's voice came over the intercom.

"Ruzak, what are you doing?"

I jerked in my chair. I startle easily, which might explain why I haven't seen a scary movie since *Aliens,* and I only saw that because of Sigourney Weaver.

"I hate November," I said, raising my voice a little, like a lot of people who use intercoms or talk to foreigners. "I've lived in Knoxville for over half my life and I can't remember one single sunny day in November."

"Maybe you should invest in a light box."

"Light box?"

"This big panel of bright light that depressed people sit in front of."

"Why do they do that?"

"Because they're depressed, Ruzak."

"No, I mean, what does the light do?"

"I'm not sure, but I think it stimulates something in their brain."

"I don't think my brain's problem is lack of stimulation."

"Probably not," she agreed. I wasn't sure why we were chatting over the intercom when she sat about twenty feet away, though we had remodeled recently, adding a wall and a door, turning the one big room into two smaller rooms. Felicia had said a detective needs privacy when consulting with his clients about their case. I suspected it had more to do with a secretary's need for privacy when consulting with her boyfriend about their lunch plans. But that was cynical thinking, and I was at war with cynical thinking, the chief reason for half the world's problems, in my opinion. You have to trust that most people act in good faith. Otherwise, you might as well build your bunker, stock up on the canned goods, and invest in the kind of firepower Sigourney used against the mother alien in the sequel. One of the things I couldn't understand in that movie was all the slobber. Those creatures seemed very insectlike to me, and I didn't think insects salivated. Of course, they weren't real monsters and it was only a movie.

"Now what are you doing?" she asked.

"Wondering if insects salivate."

"You know, that's really weird. I was just wondering the same thing."

"Really?" It would be an extraordinary coincidence if she were. "Well, I know mosquitoes have spit. They inject it into the bite to facilitate blood flow."

"Ruzak, only you could get from light boxes to mosquito spit in ten seconds."

I didn't think she was paying me a compliment. I asked, "What's going on?" which was more polite than saying, "Why are you hassling me over this damned intercom?"

"There's somebody here to see you."

I didn't think I had any appointments, so I asked, "Do they have an appointment?"

"He says he doesn't need one."

My heart rate clicked up a notch. People who don't need appointments are not usually the kind of people you want to meet with.

"Okay, show him in."

The door opened and I recognized him right away, with the square-shaped head, the ill-fitting suit, the slight paunch and rounded shoulders. I could see Felicia over his shoulder making a slicing motion across her throat and I nodded toward her, saying, "Thanks, Felicia, I'll take it from here."

He sat in the chair in front of my desk, I sat in the chair behind my desk, and he was smiling with great satisfaction.

"Mr. Ruzak, do you remember me?" he asked.

"Oh," I said. "You bet I do. I've always been pretty good with faces. Sometimes I have trouble remembering names, but one look at a face and I've got it locked down. I still remember what my ninth-grade art teacher looked like. Can I get you anything? We've got practically everything, even Starbucks coffee."

"No thank you," he said, crossing his legs and setting his briefcase on his lap.

"You sure? Once a week, my secretary picks up a pound. That way I avoid the lady on the cup."

"What lady?"

"You know, the creepy Starbucks lady. Although she is on the bag too, but it's usually my secretary who makes the coffee, so I don't have to look at her."

"You don't have to look at your secretary?"

"Oh, I don't mind that. I was talking about the Starbucks lady."

His smile had fled. "I don't know what you're talking about, Mr. Ruzak."

"She's on all the cups. Check it out next time you're at Starbucks."

"I don't go to Starbucks."

"Well, it is an acquired taste, like beer."

He shook his head quickly, as if he were clearing out the cobwebs, and said, "You must know why I'm here, Mr. Ruzak."

"I've got a pretty strong suspicion, Mr. Hilton."

"Hinton."

"Hinton. Hinton. That's right. Sorry."

He pulled a computer printout from his briefcase. "Mr. Ruzak, I've brought your test results. . . ."

"Okay," I said. "I've already seen them. I know you didn't come looking for excuses, but I was never very good with tests."

"I," he said, "don't care."

"I didn't think so. I don't suppose you looked carefully at my door before you came in. Right below the 'Highly Effective Detection' name thingy? 'Theodore Ruzak, Investigative Consultant.' We added that so potential clients wouldn't confuse me with your traditional detective-type setup."

"Your clients might be confused, Mr. Ruzak. And, based on your test results, you are most definitely confused. But the state of Tennessee is not confused. All applicants must pass this test in order to obtain the license to practice private detection."

"And that's a good thing," I said. "You wouldn't want just any yahoo dicking around with detection, private or otherwise."

"No, we do not."

"Well, I'm already signed up for the next test, and this time I've got high hopes of passing it. My problem was I didn't sleep well the night before, and this time I'm planning to take a pill. Not a prescription, but something over-the-counter."

"That's entirely up to you, Mr. Ruzak."

"Well, that's a relief and one of the reasons this is such a great country, Mr. Hilton. Hillon. Hellion. *Hinton*. Multiple shots at the target."

"Right. And while you're reloading . . ." He pulled a document from his briefcase and slid it across the blotter toward me.

"What's this?" I asked. My name was in all caps in the left-hand corner, like this: THEODORE RUZAK d/b/a THE HIGHLY EFFECTIVE DETECTION AND INVESTIGATION COMPANY a/k/a "THE DIC". Above it was this: THE STATE OF TENNESSEE VS.

"A cease-and-desist order, Mr. Ruzak. Effective immediately, you are no longer in business."

"Wow. Just like that?"

He was smiling at me like every villain in every B movie I've ever seen. If he'd had a mustache, he'd have twirled it.

"Just like that," he said.

"You know, I'm not much for irony, but this strikes me as ironic."

"How so?"

"Up till this minute I was making a living off the fact that people do bad things and haven't answered for them, and here you are shutting me down."

"I don't see the irony in that."

"Well, like I said."

"I understand from your application you used to be a night watchman. Perhaps you could apply for that job."

"Does career counseling come with your work?" I asked. "That part of the service?"

"There's no need for bitterness, Mr. Ruzak."

"I guess not in general. But this is a particular case." I was regretting offering him the coffee. "I was thinking about the movies before you came in. If this was a movie and I was your typical hard-case gumshoe, I'd tear up this court order and throw the pieces back into your face."

"I'm a lucky man, then, that you are neither hard-case nor a gumshoe."

He stood up. I stayed down. Felicia appeared in my doorway.

"So that's it?" she asked. She was looking over Hinton's shoulder at me. "That's all you're gonna do?"

"You have to the end of business today, Mr. Ruzak," Hinton said, tipping his hat in my direction before slipping it on his square head. "Or I come back with the Knox County Sheriff's Department."

He left. Felicia sat in the chair he vacated and stared at me.

"I flunked the test," I told her.

"You never told me you flunked the test."

"I meant to. Okay, that's a lie. What I meant to do was take it again and hope for the best."

I braced myself for the explosion. But all she did was drop a piece of paper on top of the court order.

"What's this?"

"What's left in the bank account."

"Really? I thought we had more than that."

"That's what we have." She crossed her arms over her chest and waited.

"Okay," I said. "But let's not jump the gun here. The next test is coming up in a couple of months. There's enough here to cover both our expenses till then. Think of it as a paid vacation."

"You're such a . . ." She searched for the word.

"Dumb-ass?"

"No."

"Mediocrity?"

"Uh-uh."

"Ne'er-do-well?"

"*Optimist*. What's the plan in two months when you flunk it a third time and all the money's gone?"

"It's hard for me to plan for failure."

"That's really strange coming from you, Ruzak. You would think that'd be second nature by now."

She spun out of the chair and was gone, slamming my door behind her. No more than thirty seconds later—time to grab her purse, maybe—I heard the outer door slam.

Alone with my thoughts—and my ferns, which were slightly droopy, making me wonder if I had them too close to the cold windows—I stared out into the alley below, into a world bled colorless by the rain, at the jumble of old filing cabinets and bent metal trash cans and dead stalks of weeds glistening in the rain. They say even the greatest minds suffered from melancholy, though I wasted another minute or two trying to think of a single genius who suffered from the blues. Lincoln, maybe, though he'd had a bit more on his plate than I did.

A voice cried out from the wilderness of the vestibule.

"Hello? Hello, is anybody home?"

I sighed. I knew that voice. I opened my door and Eunice Shriver shuffled in, wearing a wool overcoat speckled with rain and carrying a canvas tote. She plopped her eighty-plus self into one of my chairs and waited for me to sink into my leather executive chair, which had developed a squeak and, as I sank, I wondered if that might affect its resale value.

"Theodore," she said, "you do not look well."

"It's this weather," I said. "You know, rainy days and Mondays."

"Rainy days and Mondays?"

"Always get me down. It's a song."

"I do not listen to the rap music or that abhorrent hip-hop."

"Neither do I. That song's pretty old."

"Meaning I should know it since I am, too?"

"No, meaning it predates rap and hip-hop by at least a generation."

"Theodore Ruzak." She sniffed. "Music critic."

"More an aficionado than a critic, Eunice. I struggle against judgmentalism."

"'Judgmentalism'? Is that a word?"

"I don't know. I'm no lexicographer." I almost added I was no detective, either, but that bordered on bitterness and self-pity. Our reactions to personal catastrophe are minefields to be gingerly navigated. I wondered if I had read that somewhere, or if it was original. Sometimes I thought things I ascribed to myself only to find out days or weeks later that somebody else said it about a hundred years ago.

"Every time I see you we spin off on tangents, Theodore," she said, waving her mottled, big-knuckled hand in a circular motion, to demonstrate a tangent.

"Well, like the poet said, the truth lies in the parentheses."

"What poet?"

"I don't know."

"Then how do you know he said it?"

"Well, I may not know who said, 'Ask not what your country . . .' But that doesn't mean it wasn't said, Eunice."

"Kennedy said that."

"I know."

"Then why did you say you didn't?"

"I didn't say I didn't. I was making a point."

"Well, perhaps there's a first time for everything." Eunice was eighty-six, and I figured the weather must be wreaking havoc on her joints. Thinking about her aching joints relieved some of the pressure in my chest—or rather moved the pressure a bit to one side, because empathy resides at a different spot than self-pity. I think the ancient Egyptians figured out that one.

"Theodore, I have come today for two reasons."

"I'll guess the first," I said. "You want to know if there's any progress on your case."

"Effective, Mr. Detective," she said. "Highly effective."

"There isn't," I told her. "Eunice, nobody is trying to kill you. People love you. They wish only the best for you."

"You are hopelessly naïve."

"Oh, you bet. But you've put me in the position of trying to prove a negative."

"Have you looked into the bag boy at Fresh Market?"

"The one with the beady eyes?"

"The one with the mole. Beady Eyes was fired months ago."

"He was?"

"I made quite sure of that!"

"Well, in that case he might be holding a grudge, but bag boy is one of those professions where you can generally find work anywhere."

"One should never underestimate the maliciousness of bag boys."

"Eunice, you know what it took me a long time to learn? We're not as important as we think we are."

"And what is that supposed to mean?"

"It means believing somebody's out to get you won't make you important, and neither will confessing to crimes you didn't commit."

"I believe you just called me a liar."

"I don't think you can be a liar, per se, without the intent to deceive. Besides, even if you're right and somebody is trying to kill you, I can't do anything about it."

"And why is that?"

I told her. She accused me of making it up just to get her off my back. I showed her the court order.

"Oh, Theodore, why didn't you study?"

"That's the distressing thing. I did."

"Well, you're still young. You'll land on your feet."

I nodded. "I've got my fingers crossed there's an opening at Fresh Market."

She laughed. I'm convinced old ladies have the best-sounding laughter on earth. She picked up her tote and plopped it into her lap.

"I'm glad you told me," she said. Somehow my losing the business had lifted her spirits. Like mine, her ache must have shifted. "Because I've begun a little project that could be quite demanding on your time. And mine, too, of course."

She fumbled in the tote.

"You're knitting me a sweater," I said.

She hauled out about half a ream of typing paper and slapped it on my blotter. I read the title on the cover page: *Theodore Ruzak, The Highly Effective Detective.* It was an eye-catching title, but I managed to tear my eyes away to look at her, cheeks that rosy red of a lot of old ladies, eyes sparkling in the center of their puffy folds.

"You remember we discussed committing your story to paper some months back," she said. "I've decided to take the liberty."

"Committing my story to paper?"

"Of course, the devil is in the details, as they say, and I've reached a point in the narrative where I simply must have your input."

"You're writing my life story?" I flipped through the pages. I saw a lot of *Ruzak*s and a lot of *Eunice*s, and every now and again somebody ejaculated, as in "'That killer's as good as caught!' ejaculated Theodore." The thought of crazy old Eunice Shriver writing a book about me was flattering and unnerving at the same time. "Why?"

"To immortalize you!" she fairly shouted. "Holmes had his Watson. Marple had her Christie. Nancy Drew had her Keene. Ruzak shall have his Shriver!"

"Oh, Eunice. Eunice, that's flattering as all get-out; I'm touched, really, but—"

"There are gaps, of course. Some things that I do not know, details and conversations and other matters that only you could know. I have been focusing on our relationship for the most part, but they'll want to know more about the actual case and your secretary, I suppose, and how precisely you managed to bag the killer."

"They? Who's 'they'?"

"Why, your readers, naturally!"

"Eunice, I don't have any readers."

"You will!"

"I don't want any readers."

"Nonsense! What detective in his right mind doesn't want readers?"

"I'm not a detective."

"You were!"

"Then I'm not in my right mind." I scooped up the manu-script and held it out for her. She didn't take it. The loss in her eyes was profound, and I looked away.

"You think I'm ridiculous," she said, voice quivering.

"No."

"A silly old woman with delusions of literary grandeur."

"Of course not."

"I wrote poetry when I was younger."

I wasn't sure what that had to do with anything, but I told her that was terrific. I was impressed. And how in the world could I accuse her, of all people, of being delusional? I kept holding out the manuscript until my forearm began to ache.

"If you really feel it's necessary," I said, "I guess you could just make up the rest."

"What rest?"

"The gaps."

"But this isn't fiction, Theodore."

"It would probably work better that way," I said. "Maybe you could put under the title: 'Based on a True Story.'"

She snorted with disgust. I figured it was disgust, anyway. Is it possible to snort with something else? Is there another emotion that causes you to snort?

She leaned forward and snatched the papers from my cramp-ing fingers.

"I shall finish with or without your help, Theodore. Do you know why?"

"No. Why?"

"Because at the ripe old age of eighty-six, I have finally stumbled upon my life's calling. I shall be known to posterity as the chronicler of the great Teddy Ruzak's exploits."

She stuffed the manuscript back into the tote and pushed herself out of the chair. We argued all the way to the door. Then I gave up. What did I care if she wrote about me? You have to have purpose in your life. The fact that I had just lost mine made this painfully obvious. Loss makes a lot of things painfully obvious.

TWO

I hung around for another couple of hours, misting the ferns, changing the voice-mail message, composing a letter to my clients about "pressing circumstances," and writing a note to stick on the front door. "Temporarily Unavailable." Ever the optimist, I had no plans to close up shop for good. I had more than enough cash in the bank to last until the next go-around and now more than enough time to bone up for the test. I'm a firm believer in that old saw about try, try again. But I wondered how kindly the state of Tennessee would treat my application, seeing that it had to get a court order to shut down my illegal operation.

I shut down Felicia's computer and cut the lights. The office fell into a kind of premature twilight. I bumped down the thermostat

to sixty-five and checked to make sure the fax machine was un-
plugged. Then I hung in the doorway, one foot over the transom
and one foot in the room, jingling the keys, knowing I'd be back
but not knowing if I would ever *really* be back.

I swung the door closed and locked it. I tapped the etching after my name, INVESTIGATIVE CONSULTANT, with my index finger,
and thumped down the wooden stairs, the naked bulb dangling
above throwing my shadow against the wall, the silhouette of my
trench coat flapping in my descent like Batman's cape.

I passed the dry cleaner's on the first floor. The walls hummed
with the sound of the machines, and I could see Gustav, the German proprietor, laboring over a shirt-pressing machine. A couple
months back, Gustav had offered to do all my suits at a 20 percent discount. I had thanked him but explained I was doing my
cleaning with those in-your-dryer bags from Sam's Club. He reacted as if I had just admitted to shooting house cats for sport.

On the stoop of the Ely, I inhaled deeply and then blew out my
breath, watching the white plume roil in the cold air. Ever since I
was a kid, the phenomenon fascinated me. The rain was as fine as
the aerosol emitted from my mister, which sat upstairs on the
window ledge beside the row of ferns. What about the ferns? I
should load them into my car and take them home. But I'd have
to climb those stairs and open that door, cross through two
rooms, past my big desk and the squeaky leather chair. Maybe I'd
come back tomorrow.

I walked a half block west to the Park Rite lot that backed up to the Ely. I was parking there because I got tired hoofing it downstairs every hour to feed the meter—or trying to remember to hoof it downstairs every hour. Sometimes I got wrapped up in something or my mind strayed, and I'd find a ticket beneath my wiper. The city was gleeful about writing tickets.

The temperature wouldn't rise much above forty today, and the forecast called for freezing rain overnight. The sky was an unbroken sheet of gray. The red reflections of cars' rear lights chased their bumpers on the shimmering pavement, and their tires hissed as they passed, the water remembering the tread for a moment before the fresh rain wiped the road clean.

An old man leaned against the lamppost at the corner of Walnut and Church. Blue jeans, a ratty tan jacket, tangled, gray-streaked hair down to his shoulders, a full beard, also laced with gray, that grew past his Adam's apple, holding a scrap of cardboard where he had scrawled, "We all need a little help now and then. God Bless." He was a regular. I'd seen him almost every day since September. One block west was the main library, where the vagrants congregated year-round, sitting in the magazine area, staying warm or cool, depending on the season. The library wasn't far from the mission on Broadway, which didn't open its doors until late afternoon. If I was a vagrant (something not too far outside the realm of possibilities), I'd hoof it farther south for the winter. I'd go south until there was no south left.

At the four-way stop where Walnut met Church Avenue, I looked over at Ratty Jacket and found him looking back at me.

In that moment, I made a life-or-death decision that would change both our lives.

I rolled down the window and he trotted over, chin tucked as he ran, and I dropped the spare change from my cup holder into his calloused palm. He commanded God to bless me, and then I reached over, grabbed my floppy hat from the passenger seat, and passed it out the window to him. It was too big for his head. The rim bobbed just over his bushy eyebrows, which were shot through with gray like his hair and beard. His eyes were wide with astonishment at my generosity. He grinned, touching the brim with one gnarled finger as I pulled away. He looked seventy at least, but probably was in his sixties.

I glanced in the rearview mirror, and he was still standing in the middle of the street, head turned toward me, a distorted, tan-and-blue figure in the rain-smeared glass.

THREE

I took Kingston Pike west, through Sequoia Hills with its hundred-year-old mansions behind wrought-iron gates and the big Greek Orthodox church, not far from the synagogue and the fundamentalists' private school, past the Fresh Market where old Eunice Shriver fingered the bag boy out to get her, through the Bearden Hill area, and on the back side of the slope I turned left into the parking lot for the Humane Society. It was the only Spanish-style building I'd ever seen in Knoxville. The Spanish never had a strong presence in eastern Tennessee to my knowledge, and I always suspected the building originally housed a Mexican restaurant.

The place stank of ammonia mixed with the air freshener used to mask the stench of the ammonia. Cages lined the walls in this outer room, and the cages were occupied by cats lolling on carpet-covered ledges a couple feet above the floors of the cages. A big tabby lifted its head and blinked sleepily as I passed. My right eye twitched in response: I'm mildly allergic to cats.

The clerk (or attendant or whatever her title was) stood up and came to the counter. Maybe nineteen or twenty, with short-cropped black hair and a silver ring through her left nostril, her name was Amanda. She was a student at UT, studying philosophy. That probably helped, working at this place, which always struck me as a way station between deliverance and oblivion. She was clad completely in black: black halter that terminated an inch above her pierced navel, tight, black, hip-hugging jeans, and black combat boots. It wasn't hard for me to picture her administering the lethal dose to some unwanted animal. I didn't pretend to know much about philosophy, but what I did know didn't favor an optimistic mindset.

"Hey, Ruzak," she said, placing the paperback she had been reading facedown on the counter, folded open to keep her place. She was reading *The Bell Jar*. "What's up?"

"The state closed me down today," I said.

"Really? How come?"

"I flunked a test."

"We have an opening washing out the runs."

"I'll keep it in mind," I said. "Just wondering if you got in anything new this week."

"Let's check it out."

She grabbed a set of keys from a hook, and I followed her through the big metal door into the back wing of the building where the dogs were caged. We were greeted by a cacophony of barks, howls, whines, yips, and snarls. Some of the dogs I recognized. Butch, the pit bull, who had arrived earlier in the month and was doomed; nobody wanted to adopt a pit bull. Sassy, a Border collie with one bad eye, half shut and weeping with some kind of abscess, yellow gunk congealing in the long hair beneath her eye. Geronimo, a handsome German shepherd mix with a nasty disposition, though that might have sprung from an intense hatred of his confinement. Some dogs poked their snouts against the wire mesh, spittle flying from their mouths, furious; others cowered in the back of their cage, heads lowered, tongues dangling, like winded sprinters. Amanda must have recently washed down the cages: the concrete floor was slick, and the steel drain covers glistened with moisture.

"Okay!" she shouted over the bedlam. We had reached the end of the row. "He's new. That one just came in last night. And that one over there, she's new. It's a she, right? Yeah."

I peered into the cages, one by one. The dogs watched me. Amanda watched them watch me, and then she watched me, thin, pale arms folded over her small chest.

"Can I ask you something, Ruzak?" she asked. "For six weeks you've been coming here, and I take you back here and you stare at these dogs and then you come back and stare some more, and you haven't even asked to take one out. What are you looking for?"

"The right dog."

"Why don't we do this? You tell me what breeds you're interested in, and, when one comes in, I'll give you a call."

"Well, it's not the breed exactly. I mean, I'm not partial to any particular breed. I've always believed in the saying that the perfect dog finds you."

"I've never heard that saying."

"It's all a little academic anyway. My lease doesn't allow pets."

"Then why are you looking for one?"

I didn't say anything. She was still watching me. The dogs were still watching me. I stood with my hands stuffed into my overcoat pockets.

"Maybe it isn't the dog you're looking for, per se," Amanda said finally.

"I have a very rich life," I told her. "An abundant existence." I wasn't about to let her existential malaise infect me. I looked into the cage immediately to my right. Some kind of low-slung beagle mix stared back. It wasn't barking, just lifting its narrow head and panting, creating the illusion of a grin. I pointed at it.

"Can I see him?"

"Sure. Go straight through that door into the courtyard and I'll bring him out. His name's Archie."

I sat on a concrete bench under the bare, outstretched arms of a dogwood, the branches black from the rain. The water gathered at the ends and formed droplets that hung, quivering, before gravity took them down. Amanda came out after a few minutes, cradling the beagle, which she lowered to the ground about ten feet from the bench. Archie looked up at her, his thin tail a white-and-tan blur, bouncing off her shins with his front paws. Amanda clapped her hands and pointed toward me, and Archie took off, leaping onto my lap and placing his tongue beneath my chin. I could smell his breath and suddenly I was twelve again, playing with my first and only dog. I'd never fully recovered from that dog's death, but I always told myself that was because you never fully recover from death, even the ones that aren't your own. Nearly a year had passed since my mom died, and I still woke up some mornings with a hard nugget of grief lodged in my gut. It had surprised me in the beginning; I always thought of grief as a hollow kind of feeling, but real grief isn't a void; it's hard and glittering and sharp as a diamond.

Now I had muddy paw prints all over my tan overcoat and this dog was nibbling the soft flesh under my chin.

"Okay, Archie, okay," I told it. I lowered it to the ground and it immediately put its paws on my leg, begging to be back in my lap.

"He likes you," Amanda said.

"He's probably not picky."

"He's small, which is good for an apartment," she said.

"It's a moral dilemma," I said. "I signed an agreement not to bring an animal into the building, but beyond that, if I get caught I'll have to bring him back here."

"So you buy him some time. You could look at it that way."

I looked her way. She might be prettier if she went back to her natural color and ditched the hoop in her nose. She must have been freezing out here in this rain, bare-armed and bare-midriffed.

"How did you decide on philosophy as a major?" I asked her.

She shrugged. "It's interesting."

"What does somebody do with a degree in philosophy?"

"I'm prelaw."

"Oh." I thought about telling her the world probably needed more philosophers and less lawyers, but that might lead to a debate, and I didn't have the stomach or the nerve to get into a philosophical debate with a philosophy major with the personality of a lawyer.

"What's ol' Archie's story anyway?" I asked.

"Brought him in a couple days ago. No collar, no implant. Just a stray, Ruzak."

"Implant?"

"You know, some vets put in those tracking chips. GPS."

"I think I read something about that," I said. "Made me think maybe we should do that with children."

She laughed for some reason.

"He's getting cold," she said. "I better get him inside."

I followed her back into the kennel. Archie smiled at me from behind his bars. His short hair shone with moisture, and I thought of otters.

"How much time does he have?"

"It's hard to say."

"I gotta think about it."

She shrugged. I followed her to the front room. Her shoulder blades poked out her back when she hugged her arms, she was so thin. Back among the cats, I sneezed.

"You got a business card?"

I did, but no business to go with it. I scrawled my home number on the back of the card and told her I wouldn't be in the office for a while.

"But don't hold him on my account," I told her, meaning Archie. "If somebody else wants him."

"Do you? You haven't said."

"I have to think about it. One thing, I'm not sure how wise or ethical it is getting a dependent on the same day I lose my sole source of income."

I sat in my idling car in the parking lot for a few minutes, watching the drops hardly larger than pinheads kiss the glass and looking past the raindrops to the magenta façade of the building. My one-bedroom at the Sterchi would seem empty when I walked in the door. I thought I should spring for some deep-pile carpet. Hardwood floors encourage echoes.

I stopped at the Food City on the corner of Kingston Pike and Northshore, to pick up a flank steak and some black beans, and I stood in one aisle at least three minutes trying to remember if I had any rice in the pantry. If I was wrong and didn't have any rice, I'd be forced to return to the store or opt for the beans without rice, which would make me feel cheated, like I was being denied something I rightfully deserved.

It turned out I did have one bag of Success Rice left in the pantry. I set up a TV tray at the end of my bed and watched a special on global warming on the Discovery Channel while I ate, just another thirty-something bachelor eating alone in his underwear, watching television. The tray was an old one, from a set I inherited from Mom. For as long as I could remember, we ate our family dinners set up in front of the old Magnavox in the family room, so Dad wouldn't miss a minute of Walter Cronkite. Somebody had told him once he resembled Walter Cronkite, and I suspected that's why Dad was so hooked on him. Dad lacked Walter's gravitas, though. His cheeks were ruddier, too, and his nose bigger, his voice higher pitched. His voice really didn't match his size. Maybe that's why Dad wasn't the greatest salesman in the world: you saw this big, barrel-chested Walter Cronkite look-alike coming at you, and when he opened his mouth he sounded like Squeaky the Clown.

Watching the Discovery Channel convinces you of three things: The world is a wonderful, wondrous place; it's going to hell in a handbasket; and you're partially to blame. I discovered that just using my toaster pumped about a hundred tons of carbon into the atmosphere every year.

I turned off the TV after the special—just doing my part—took a shower with colder water than usual, and tried to read an online manual Felicia had printed out, before I flunked the last time, called *Passing the PI Exam, Tennessee Edition*.

I fell asleep with the thing on my chest, clutching a highlighter.

NOVEMBER 8

FOUR

*T*he phone rang a little after ten. It was Felicia.

"Did I wake you?" she asked.

I admitted she did. She asked if I had had a late night. I said I was up studying.

"See, that's what disturbs me about you, Ruzak. You studied before the last test and still flunked. Maybe you're going about this all wrong. Maybe you need some vices to overcome."

"Well," I said. "I think too much. I'm overburdened with memories. I'm extremely sensitive to loud noises and ethical quagmires, and I've got a soft heart." I told her about giving my hat to the old bum and the dog named Archie.

"I was thinking more along the lines of alcohol or gambling

or even cheap, meaningless one-night stands. You know, the stereotypical hardboiled detective thing."

"How would that help?"

"It might give you some depth."

I wasn't sure, but I thought maybe she was implying I was boring.

"I'm not a very accomplished drunk," I told her. "Some drunks are belligerent or funny or loud or sentimental. I just fall asleep."

I asked her if she wanted to have lunch. She asked if I had looked out my window. I looked out my window. The low-slung clouds had departed and the midmorning sunlight was harsh, reflecting off the rows of icicles glittering like silver thorns on the bare branches of the trees and the crystalline stalactites hanging from the power lines.

"Downtown got hit the worst," Felicia told me. "Over an inch."

"I was going to the office to pick up the ferns," I said.

"Probably best to wait till this afternoon."

"How about dinner?" I asked. "I'll take you and Tommy to Steak-N-Shake." Steak-N-Shake was Tommy's favorite.

"We'll have to take a rain check," Felicia said. "Bob's off tonight." Then she changed the subject. "I hope you're not going to spend all your time studying for this test, Ruzak. Maybe you should join a gym."

"Okay. I know I'm out of shape—"

"That's not what I meant. Or maybe one of those continuing

education classes they offer at the university. I mean, dear God, you're interested in practically everything."

"I have been thinking about a photography class," I said. "Or videography—if that's a word. You know, I could write off the cost of the class that way."

"You remember Beatrice from the diner? We were talking the other day and—"

"Don't set me up."

"I wasn't—"

"Don't try to set me up, Felicia. I don't need setting up. As a matter of fact, I've got a little more on my plate than I can handle right now."

"You're kidding."

"Why? Why do you think that's something I'd kid about? Hang on. I've got another call."

I pressed the mouthpiece against my stomach and stared out the window at the ice-gripped landscape. I had a terrific view of the railroad yard from my bedroom. On a clear day, you could see the tracks stretching far into the horizon, until they disappeared into the mists of the Smoky Mountains.

I brought the receiver back to my ear.

"You still there?" I asked. "Sorry. That was Amanda."

"Oh. Who's Amanda?"

"This girl philosopher I know."

"I'm sorry. You said . . . girl philosopher?"

"We've begun to mesh. Say, would you say it's unethical of me to adopt a dog, seeing it's forbidden on my lease, and if I get busted I probably won't get kicked out but the dog sure will?"

"You could always say you were pet-sitting."

"Well, the issue was ethics, and I'm pretty sure lying like that would be that. Unethical."

"You never mentioned any Amanda to me."

"We keep our personal lives personal, remember?"

I think I pissed her off with that remark, because she got off the phone pretty quick. I looked out the window one more time and thought Nature, like a woman, was beautiful, but treacherous . . . or maybe they were beautiful by virtue of their treachery.

"It's ironic," I said to the empty room, "that I debate ethics right in the middle of a lie about a girl calling." If I had a dog, I could talk to it and not to an empty room. If you talk to a dog, you're just being a kind owner. But talk to an empty room and you're being a weirdo.

The thought of staying inside until that afternoon was unbearable, so I dressed, pulling on an extra pair of socks ("Layers, layers, layers," my mom always lectured) and my tan overcoat with Archie's muddy prints still embossed on it, and took the elevator down to the parking lot beneath the building.

The sunlight had that late-fall-early-winter fierceness, bright but heatless, hard-edged, bordering on cruel, the way it cut the shadows of the trees and the buildings along Gay Street, and a million little suns sparkled in the ice that hung from the branches and glittered like rows of teeth belonging to some under-the-bed monster along the edges of the awnings. Nearly every building along this stretch of Gay was being renovated, into condos mostly, even the old Tennessee Theater Building, and one-bedroom lofts there were going for four hundred thousand dollars a pop.

At dawn, the salt trucks must have covered downtown, because I encountered no ice on the road on the seven-minute drive to the Ely Building. I turned left into the Park Rite lot and parked beside my building. The attendant, a guy named Lonny, left the sanctuary of his little lean-to and sauntered over as I climbed out of my Sentra.

"You're two weeks late," he informed me.

"I wanted to talk to you about that," I said. I told him I was taking a sabbatical and wouldn't be using the space for the next couple of months.

"We can't hold it," he said, meaning my space. "What's a sabbatical?"

"A working vacation."

"What are you working on?"

"I'm not, really."

"Then why'd you say you were?"

"I was trying to sound important."

He laughed and lit a cigarette. He wore a blue jacket too thin for the weather, jeans, and brown work boots. He accompanied me toward the front of the Ely, and the sand he must have shoveled earlier to clear the ice crunched beneath his boots.

"Actually, I've got to study for my PI exam," I admitted. "I just dropped by to pick up my ferns."

Smoke roiled from his nose. "I didn't know you were a PI."

"I'm not. I've got to pass the test first, hence the sabbatical."

"I'm starting trucking school in January."

"I've always admired truckers," I told him. "All those long, lonely hours behind the wheel."

"You're kidding, right?"

"I have a romantic streak."

He gave me a look, like he suspected I was trying out a pickup line on him.

"Seriously, you can't just hold my space?" I asked.

"Not unless you want to keep paying."

"I'm thinking that might be a foolish use of my funds."

"Because you might fail?"

"I'm trying to get out of that habit," I said. We had reached the front steps. I wondered how I would manage it, sitting in that little shacklike structure for eight hours with nobody to talk to. It probably wouldn't be hard for me at all—before I almost became a detective, I had worked fourteen years on the nightshift as a security guard, sitting in an armless chair, watching video monitors showing empty halls.

"What habit?" he asked. His hands belonged to an older man, the skin bunched tight around the knuckles, fingers stained by tobacco, slightly red from the cold.

"The habit of planning for failure instead of success. I like to think of myself as an optimist, but sometimes the evidence points the other way."

"I could talk to the boss about holding it," he said. Back to the real issue at hand.

"Hey, I'd appreciate that, Lonny."

We stood in silence for a second, then he said, "S'posed to warm up this afternoon. Toppin' forty-five."

"At least the sun finally came out," I said.

"Yeah-a. He lifted his face, turning it slightly to the left to bathe in the light. "Gotta enjoy it while you can."

I thanked him again and went up the narrow stairwell to my office. Yesterday's mail lay on the floor and I scooped it up. Bills. I unlocked Felicia's desk, grabbed the checkbook, and sat behind my desk. I wrote the checks, stuffed the envelopes, and then got up and started a pot of Starbucks coffee, turning the bag around so I wouldn't have to look at the lady. While I waited for the coffee to brew, I hunted for some stamps, but came up dry. I went back to my desk and drank my coffee. When two-thirds of it was inside me, I got up again (I never drain the dregs; I don't know why) and filled my mister from the bathroom tap. The sunlight could not penetrate into the alley; the arc of the sun was too low this time of year.

I was leaning over the wide ledge, misting the final fern, when something caught my eye in the alley below. My finger froze on the trigger. I brought my face closer to the window. My breath fogged the glass and I couldn't see. I wiped the moisture away with my shirtsleeve and peered again into the narrow space. It was a trick of light below, in the jumble of refuse crowded against the wall of the building behind me; it had to be. I threw the latch and, grunting with the effort because the window must have been literally painted shut, heaved the thing open, bending over the fern so the outstretched tips tickled my Adam's apple, and squinted two stories down, into the face of a dead man, wearing ratty old jeans and a brown jacket, with a beard encrusted with ice and eyes staring up into mine, unblinking and wide with horror.

FIVE

I dialed 911, and after I dialed 911 I dialed Felicia's number.

"There's a dead body in the alley," I told her.

A second of silence, then: "What alley?"

"The alley behind the Ely." I tipped my cup and the lukewarm coffee caressed the tip of my tongue. "I think it's the panhandler."

"What panhandler?"

"The one I gave my hat to yesterday."

"Are you sure?"

"Sure there's a body or sure it's the guy from yesterday? Pretty sure about both."

"Ruzak, are you okay?"

"I'm a little shaky. I shouldn't be drinking coffee on an empty stomach. I wanted some Krispy Kremes but I was afraid of black ice."

"Black ice."

"You know, that ice on the road you can't see and all of sudden you're spinning out of control at forty-five miles per hour. So I drove straight to work and I was misting the ferns before I lugged them downstairs to my car, though I probably shouldn't have done that. They're heavier now with fresh water, but if I hadn't I wouldn't have seen the dead body. Well, I don't know for a hundred percent certain that he's dead, which raises a conundrum. If he's dead, I think there's a good chance that's a crime scene down there and I don't want to muck up any evidence. But if he's alive, I have a moral responsibility to do everything I can to save him."

"Did you call the cops?"

"They're on their way."

"You want me to come down there? You don't sound right."

"I'm okay. He has my hat, though."

"Your hat?"

"Yeah, I gave him my big floppy hat yesterday . . . protection from the elements." I gave a dry, little laugh. "Anyway, I'm gonna have to explain why he has my hat."

"Ruzak, I don't have a sitter for Tommy or I'd—"

"No, I'm okay, really." I wondered what happened to Bob. She had said Bob had the day off. Maybe she didn't like to leave Tommy alone with Bob—but why wouldn't Felicia like that? Maybe Bob got called in on a fire emergency. That sounded redundant to me. Weren't all fires emergencies? My head began to hurt.

"Are you there?" she asked.

I told her I was.

"I'll stay on till the cops get there."

"No, really, that's okay. I just called to let you know. I better get down there."

"Don't touch anything, Ruzak."

"Why would I do that?" I snapped. Then I said, "Sorry. It's the damn coffee. I'll talk to you later."

I hung up, slung my coat over my shoulders, and pounded down the stairs and onto the sidewalk, turning left into the parking lot, and Lonny came out of his little shack, a cigarette dangling from the corner of his mouth.

"Where's the ferns?" he asked.

"Upstairs," I answered. He fell into step beside me as I marched toward the back of the building. The sun actually felt warm against my back. I stopped at the southwest corner of the Ely and turned to Lonny.

"I'm ninety-nine percent certain there's a dead body in that alley," I said. He blinked at me a couple of times.

"You're shittin' me."

"I've already called the cops."

He stood behind me as I pivoted to look into the alley. A wrought-iron gate blocked the entrance, but the gate's latch was broken and it hung open about a foot. Five feet in, the man lay crumpled against an old rusting filing cabinet, legs draped over a black plastic trash bag that had broken open, his face with its glittering ice mask craning upward, as if he were looking at the bright blue ribbon of cloudless sky between the buildings.

"You think he's really dead?" Lonny whispered.

"I don't see him breathing," I said.

"Exposure, poor bastard," he said. "The cold must've killed him."

I had seen dark marks on his forehead from my window, but at street level, with his head thrown back, my angle was bad. They looked like some kind of hieroglyphics from two stories above, but I didn't think so. I didn't think anyone had scribbled hieroglyphics on his forehead. I stepped into the little opening between the gate and the wall of the Ely, raising my hands so I wouldn't touch anything, and rose to my tiptoes. I lost my balance and stumbled forward. Lonny clawed at my overcoat, trying to catch me before I tripped and landed flat on my face, but he missed. I didn't fall, though. I found my balance and now, with only a couple of feet separating me from the body, I could see clearly what someone had written on his forehead.

YHWH.

"What is it, Ruzak?" Lonny, hovering at the gate, hissed at me.

"Letters," I said, lowering my voice and not sure why. "*Y-h-w-h.*"

"*Y-h-w-h?* What's it mean?"

His arms were flung straight out from his sides, and he

clutched in his right hand the scrap of cardboard I saw the day before: *We all need a little help now and then. God Bless.* I didn't see my hat.

"Hey, I know that guy!" Lonny said. "I had to run him off the lot a couple times."

Where was my hat? "What's his name?" I asked.

"No clue, man."

I shuffled backward, out of the alley, and Lonny lit a cigarette. He held out the pack and I shook my head.

"Somebody told me I need more vices, but I smoked one time when I was thirteen and it made my brain feel like Swiss cheese."

"Swiss cheese. Right." Lonny's hands were quivering.

"And every time I drink I get very sleepy. Not so much with beer, though."

"Once I drank a fifth of bourbon and put my head through a wall."

"A solid wall?"

"Drywall. So it didn't hurt much."

"People used to use it as an anesthetic."

"People still do."

We waited for the sirens. I turned away from the dead man in the alley. It felt like the watched-pot phenomenon.

"You see any blood?" he asked.

"No."

"Got drunk, passed out, and froze to death."

"Before or after somebody wrote on his forehead?"

"Maybe he wrote on it himself."

"I gave him my hat," I said. "Just yesterday."

I lifted my face toward the cloudless sky. The Discovery Channel had shown examples of my carbon output as big black blocks, each block representing a certain amount of greenhouse gas, pouring into the atmosphere in choking abundance. This November sky made that difficult to believe. But if science has taught us anything since Galileo, it's taught us you can't always trust your senses. Ever since I heard about it, I was troubled by the string theory in physics. I didn't pretend to understand everything about it, or even a hundredth of it, but the thrust of the argument that there might be an infinite number of equally plausible universes, that reality as I knew it wasn't the only reality, had cost me at least six hours of sleep, cumulatively. I was relieved to read that the string theory was falling out of favor with some highly placed eggheads, one of them saying that it didn't even rise to the level of being wrong.

"Why'd you give him your hat?"

"It was raining."

I looked down at Lonny. He was at least a foot shorter. He was looking up at me.

"What's your dog's name?" he asked, nodding toward the stains on my coat.

"I don't have a dog."

"You give him that, too?"

"I went to the pound and met a beagle named Archie."

"I would have taken you for a cat man."

"I'm allergic."

"I'm allergic to shellfish."

"I saw this show on . . . well, I can't remember now, but it was one of the networks, about this woman who was allergic to her own sweat. She basically suffered from an autoimmune response to her own body."

"You gotta wonder why something like that happens," Lonny said. He flicked his cigarette into the lot, where it bounced and rolled until it hit the front wheel of my car.

"Genetics," I said. "DNA."

"I'm talkin' about God."

"Oh. Right."

"You believe in God, Ruzak?"

"I was raised Southern Baptist," I said. "My old man was a lapsed Catholic."

"I'm a Methodist, but I haven't been to church in fifteen years."

"I can't approach the whole thing like a child, you know, like Jesus said to somebody, I think in the Temple. It definitely wasn't the Mount . . . anyway, I think too much, which tends to keep the profound things at arm's length—sort of the opposite of what you'd expect."

We heard the sirens approaching. Lonny lit another cigarette.

"If he was a goddamned banker, he'd be at Fort Sanders by now with a drip going," he said.

The first responder was a truck from the Knoxville Fire Department. Two guys jumped out, neither of whom were named Bob. Lonny and I stood behind the gate and watched them check the old man's vital signs. One EMT felt for a pulse while the other shone a light into his eyes.

"He's gone," the guy with the light announced. He sported a bushy mustache. You don't see many men over thirty with facial hair these days, and those you do see usually practice one of those macho professions or have no profession at all, like the dead man in the alley with YHWH tattooed on his forehead. Maybe it *was* a tattoo and I just didn't notice it the day before.

An ambulance pulled into the lot and, while they were unfolding the gurney, a cop car parked behind my back bumper. The cop's name was Middleton. He took our statements while they carried the body through the gate (the gurney was too wide to fit through the opening). They had to turn the old guy sideways to get him out because he had gone stiff, and his arms remained outstretched as if he had fallen frozen in an attitude of flight.

I told Middleton about my encounter with the deceased the day before and how I discovered him in the alley. Lonny didn't have much to add, except the fact that he had seen him off and on for over three months and once had to chase him out of the parking lot.

No, we didn't know his name. No, we didn't know where he came from or how long he had been working Church Avenue.

No, we had never seen him with anyone else. No, there didn't seem to be anything wrong when I gave him my hat.

"Why did you give him your hat?" Middleton asked.

"It was raining."

They had loaded up the body into the ambulance by this point. They slammed the back doors, sauntered to the front, and the ambulance slowly and silently pulled out of the parking lot. It seemed odd and disquieting. No crowd had gathered, either, as you might expect. The sidewalk was deserted and it was nearing lunchtime. Middleton scribbled in his pad. We followed him into the alley. He touched the piece of cardboard with the toe of his shiny black shoe.

"That's his," I said. "He was holding that yesterday."

Middleton threw a leg over the rusting filing cabinet and walked to the opposite corner of the Ely, head turning back and forth as he scanned the ground. I turned the opposite way, to poke about near the gate for my hat. What happened to my hat? Did he give it to somebody? Did he lay it down somewhere and forget about it? Except for the handmade sign, there was nothing else I could see as evidence of the old man dying here—or even having been alive here. No discarded liquor bottles, no cigarette butts, no bag of belongings. Hadn't I seen a backpack resting against the stop sign on Walnut?

Middleton returned, broken glass crunching under his polished shoes. He was just a kid, no more than twenty-one or two,

I guessed. At that age, I had already flunked out of the police academy and been denied readmittance.

"Got drunk, passed out, and froze to death," Middleton said, echoing Lonny from a few minutes ago. He flipped his notebook closed. "But we'll see what the coroner says."

"You see the letters?"

"What letters?"

"The letters tattooed or etched on his forehead."

He gave me a look. I had left that out in my statement, so I told him what I saw. He didn't bother to write it down.

"Okay, one more thing. I'm gonna need your names and numbers, in case there's anything hinky in the ME's report."

It turned out Lonny's last name was Bradford, like the fruitless pear trees that grew so abundantly in East Tennessee. Middleton paused after writing down my name.

"Ruzak. The detective, right?"

"Not anymore. Well, actually, not ever."

"He's on sabbatical," Lonny offered.

"I remember seeing your name in the paper," Middleton said.

He drove away and, after he drove away, Lonny lit another cigarette.

"You wanna grab some lunch?" he asked me.

I hadn't even had breakfast, but I told him no. I wanted to get my ferns home. For some reason, I was feeling very protective toward them.

SIX

Felicia had left a message on my answering machine, so after I ate a pimento cheese sandwich, I called her back.

"He's definitely dead," I told her.

"What happened?"

"They think he passed out drunk and froze to death."

"That's sad."

"I didn't see a bottle, though. And my hat's missing."

"Foul play, Ruzak? Somebody killed him for your hat? I've seen that hat. It's not that nice. Why did you give him your hat in the first place?"

"Because it was raining."

"Maybe another bum stumbled over him and took your hat. And his bottle."

"That could be. Are you busy later?"

"I'm going out of town."

"You are? You didn't tell me."

"Sorry, Mom."

"Where are you going?"

"I'm taking Tommy to Kentucky for a couple of weeks to visit with his grandparents."

"What about Bob?"

"What about him? Why are you always so worried about Bob's whereabouts?"

"I'm not."

"Well, you're sure making inquiries all the time. Bob has to work, if you must know."

"That should be a nice trip," I said. "Watch for ice, though. Especially around Jellico Mountain."

"That's on my list, Ruzak."

I told her about the letters on the bum's forehead.

"What do you think that means?" I asked.

"What the letters mean or what it means that they were on his forehead?"

"Either one."

She had no idea. Neither did I. We mulled over in silence for a few seconds our mutual lack of any idea.

"Are you still there?" I asked.

"Yes, but I gotta go. Tommy wants lunch."

"I just had a pimento cheese sandwich."

"O-*kay*. . . . Ruzak, are you trying to keep me on the phone for some reason?"

"I guess I could be a little spooked. I think I would be okay if he had died with his eyes closed. You know, I look down and there he is, staring at me."

"He wasn't really staring, you know."

"Or if somebody else found him," I went on. "I know this sounds egocentric and I have a problem with that, but it feels like, I don't know, that he was meant for me."

"*What?*"

"The day before the state shuts me down, and I didn't tell you about the cop, but he reminded me of me, except he obviously graduated from the Academy, and then I gave him my hat—not the cop, the bum—and it feels like I'm coming to some sort of epiphany or reaching a kind of existential critical mass—one of those moments when you can hear the muffled strike of the hammer."

"Hammer?"

"You know, the hammer of Fate with a capital H."

"I think you're reading too much into the whole thing. Some homeless man freezes to death and you happen to be the one who finds him."

I could hear Tommy shouting in the background, an incoherent, desperate sound. Tommy was Felicia's kid by a guy who ran out on her when she was pregnant, and there were problems with the kid. I could picture him, tugging on her clothes, his wide face twisted into a grimace.

"You have to go," I said.

"I have to go. Don't have a crisis on me, Ruzak. Maybe you should get out of town, too. Go someplace warm for a while."

That's it, I thought after I hung up. That's what was getting to me, besides the letters on his forehead and the way he seemed to be staring at me. Why didn't he get to some place warm? The mission would have been open, and I knew for a fact that the Catholic church on Northshore kept its doors unlocked 24/7. If he passed out drunk, why didn't we find a bottle in the alley? Of course, he might have died of a heart attack or stroke or any number of other causes. Maybe he had pneumonia or cancer or some other, more exotic disease. There are so many things that can kill you; it's amazing we live past forty.

I tried to tell myself it wasn't because of those letters on his forehead or my own moribund mindset or the nature of my former business that convinced me—absolutely convinced me beyond all doubt—that that old man had been murdered and left in that alley as if he were just another bit of refuse, another bag of garbage.

NOVEMBER 15

SEVEN

I noticed a tall, pale-skinned, dark-haired woman standing on the steps of the Sterchi Building as I turned into the parking lot. She was wearing a calf-length gray overcoat with matching gray gloves. She reminded me of your classic femme fatale from those old Humphrey Bogart movies. Thin, seductive, soft-spoken . . . and deadly.

I pulled into my space and saw her walking toward me, and even her makeup made me think I'd stumbled into a Philip Marlowe story: her lips were the color of arterial blood.

"Teddy Ruzak?" she asked. Her heels were gray, too, and their clicking echoed in the confines of the underground garage.

I told her I was. She flashed a badge and said, "Detective Meredith Black, Mr. Ruzak. Knoxville Homicide."

"It's the old man in the alley," I said. "Somebody killed him."

"I'm afraid so."

"I knew it."

"Do you have a few minutes? I've been trying to reach you by phone . . ."

"I was meeting with my biographer. Sure. You want me to come downtown?"

"This won't take long. Can we talk upstairs?"

She meant my apartment. Immediately I thought about the dishes piled in the sink and the view through my open bedroom door: the dirty socks, the pile of newspapers, the collection of coffee mugs on my nightstand.

"Sure. That's no problem."

We took the elevator to the third floor, and she stood a couple steps behind me as I fumbled with the keys. I always got nervous around cops. Cops and pretty women. And big dogs. Closed spaces. Dark, unfamiliar locales. Bikers. Certain members of the clergy. Like a priest is much more intimidating to me than a Protestant minister.

"I've been meaning to tidy up," I said over my shoulder as I stepped inside. The blinds were drawn and the place had all the light and charm of an Egyptian tomb. I flipped on a light and went immediately to the sink, glancing down the little hall to the bedroom. The door was not fully open, so maybe she wouldn't notice.

"Can I get you anything?" I asked. "Water, but it's tap, sorry, or I could make a fresh pot of coffee. . . ."

"No, thanks," Meredith Black said. She was kind of hovering near the door as if she were waiting for something, and I guessed that something was for me to gather my thoughts and start acting like a normal, innocent human being.

"Let me take your coat," I said.

"Thanks." She shrugged the coat into my hands. Underneath she was wearing a gray jacket over a crisp white blouse. A diamond solitaire hung around her neck on a sterling silver chain. Without thinking, I checked out her left hand. No ring. I draped her overcoat carefully over the back of a bar chair and motioned her toward the sofa.

"So you knew it was murder?" Meredith Black said. She left the *how?* unspoken.

"Well, when I said I knew, I didn't mean I knew."

She smiled. She had good teeth. Very white and straight. You could tell a lot about people based on the condition of their teeth. Socioeconomic status. Their sense of self-worth. Their personality type. In life, there are biters and there are chewers. Meredith Black, I was guessing, was a biter.

"It just didn't make much sense to me," I said. "The idea that he just passed out and froze to death. Of course, I'm no doctor and even if I was, I didn't examine him or anything. I didn't even touch him. I figured it could have been a heart attack or a stroke, but I had this gut feeling, based on a couple of factors, that nothing natural killed him."

"What factors?" She was leaning forward, chin thrust forward, elbows on her knees. Her knuckles were red, a little chafed, probably from the cold.

"I didn't think he was new to the, um, lifestyle, which meant he knew where to go to survive the cold. I guess I should tell you right off I had an encounter with him the day before. It was raining and I gave him some change—and my hat. My hat was missing, and people like him don't toss a perfectly good hat. But I may have thought that because the hat had been mine and we tend to inflate the value of our possessions. . . . sorry; I ramble when I'm nervous."

"Why are you nervous?"

"I kind of lost my job a couple weeks ago and, you know, that sort of thing can yank the rug right out from under you, and I don't mean just in the financial sense."

She nodded. "Sure. You were a PI, right?"

"Investigative consultant. Never quite reached the PI level, which is what led me to lose my job. The state didn't grasp the nuance."

She reviewed the statement I gave to Officer Middleton. How I found the body and if I had seen anything or anyone suspicious that morning or the day before when I handed the old guy my hat. How often I had seen him hanging on the corner panhandling. She wanted to know what we said to each other when he came to my car.

"I didn't say anything. He said 'God bless,' or something like that. That's it."

"Where did you go next?"

"Where did I go? I went to the pound."

"The pound?"

"The Humane Society down on Kingston Pike. I'm kind of in the market for a dog. It's still in the planning stages because I've got a lease issue. There's a philosophy student named Amanda who works there." I realized she wanted to know my alibi. "Then I went home. No. First I stopped at Food City and picked up dinner. Flank steak and beans. Black beans. I came home and ate in my bedroom. Not that I normally eat in my bedroom, but the hardwood in here makes the kitchen area kind of echoey. . . . And the next morning, the morning I found him, the only reason I went downtown was to retrieve those ferns over there. I wasn't planning on going into the office for the next couple of months, and I didn't want them to die." I told her about seeing his face, calling 911, and then calling Felicia before going downstairs.

"Felicia?"

"My secretary. She's not here. I don't mean *here* here. We aren't . . . she doesn't . . . we don't . . . She's in Kentucky visiting her parents."

"Okay. So after you tell Felicia, you go downstairs and meet . . ." She consulted her notebook. "Lonny Bradford?"

"Right. Lonny. Only I didn't know his last name till the dead guy turned up. I never asked. That happens a lot in the service sector. You know, everyone's on a first-name basis."

"What else do you know about Lonny?"

"Is he a suspect?"

She didn't answer. She just smiled at me with those bright, even teeth. Biter.

"Well, not much," I said. "He's studying to be a long-haul trucker. Or going to study for it. The only other thing I've got is my impression of him, which is he's a pretty nice guy. Oh, and he's a Methodist."

"A Methodist?" She wrote that down.

"What are you, Mr. Ruzak?"

"What am I?" The question was so open-ended I didn't even know where to start.

"Methodist, Baptist, Episcopal?"

"I guess you could call me a lapsed Baptist. My mother was keen on that, but it never quite took with me. My father was a nonpracticing Catholic. He dropped the whole thing when he married my mom, but it's one of those things you can never really get away from. The minute he realized he was dying, he demanded to see a priest. Even then, though, I suspected he was hedging his bets. The sad fact is it's more the terror of death than the joy of life that drives us to God."

"That's very interesting, Mr. Ruzak."

"Can I ask why all this matters?"

"We think whoever killed him also wrote those letters on his forehead."

"*Y-h-w-h.*"

She nodded. "Yes."

"That was the other factor that made me think this was a crime. What do they mean?"

"YHWH is the tetragrammaton, Mr. Ruzak. The four-letter, unpronounceable name of God."

EIGHT

The old guy's name was John Minor, Cadillac Jack, or sometimes just Cadillac to those who knew him on the street or at the mission on Broadway, where he ate most of his meals. He had a record. Vagrancy. Trespassing. One count of B&E: he had served two years of a suspended sentence in Bushy State Prison for jimmying the lock of a package store on Middlebrook Pike. No one Meredith Black had talked to could say exactly when John Minor showed up in Knoxville, why he came, or where he had come from. He was a loner and rarely talked about himself or his past. He claimed to have served some time in the military, but so far they hadn't found any record of his service. He said he had no family. He'd been tested at Bushy Mountain, and diagnosed as mildly retarded. That was all anyone seemed to know about Cadillac Jack.

"How did he die?" I asked.

"He was beaten to death, Mr. Ruzak."

"And you think the killer might be some kind of religious fanatic or something?"

"Did you notice the letters when you gave him your hat?"

"No, but it was raining and the whole exchange lasted about thirty seconds. I could have missed it."

"No one who knew him can remember seeing them before," she said. "And nobody remembers him being particularly religious."

"Down on Market Square there's that homeless preacher guy, you know the one? He stands on the corner shouting Bible verses and promising eternal damnation to everybody who ignores him."

She nodded. "I know who you're talking about."

"Maybe you oughta talk to him."

She smiled. Perfect teeth always reminded me of my own drawbacks in the orthodontics department: I have a slight overbite and those stubborn stains on the canines.

"We just might do that," she said. She had put away her notebook. The interview was over. She shot up from the sofa—there's no other way to describe it, she rose so fast—and extended her hand with those pink, raw-looking knuckles.

"Thank you for your time, Mr. Ruzak."

"Oh, you can call me Teddy."

"Thank you, Teddy. And I'm Meredith."

"Meredith, that's terrific," I said.

"If you can think of anything else . . ." She handed me her card.

I dug in my wallet for one of mine.

"I don't need that," she said.

"No? No, I guess you wouldn't." I put it back in my wallet, my face flushed, like a guy rejected in a pickup bar. Her perfume was of the musky variety. She also seemed awfully young to have made detective; she looked like she was still in her twenties.

I gave her coat back and, on the way to the door, she said, "So you live alone, Mr. Ruzak?"

"One of the reasons I was at the pound that day," I said. "Now that my doors are shut I'm spending a lot more time here and there's only so much TV I can take."

"I have two dogs, Wally and Beaver."

"I loved that show when I was a kid," I said. I started to tell her my favorite character wasn't the Beav or Wally but Lumpy, the fat kid next door, but thought she might interpret that as my identifying with Lumpy because of his size. I didn't want to draw attention to mine, and the fact was I had no idea why I liked Lumpy. Too much time had passed. "What breed?"

"Dobermans."

Probably the only Dobermans on earth with the names Wally and Beaver. We shook hands again at the door.

"We'll be in touch," she promised, and was gone before I could ask the question that immediately leapt to mind.

Why?

Amanda called that afternoon. From work, according to my caller ID. I assumed she was calling about Archie. I was wrong.

"The cops just called me," she said.

"Detective Black," I said.

"I don't remember her name. Some transient was murdered in your alley?"

"Well, it's not *my* alley, per se. She's just being thorough, checking out my alibi."

"So you knew this guy?"

"No, not really. I gave him my hat that day. I thought you might be calling about Archie."

"No, I was calling to tell you the cops are checking you out."

"I don't take it personally. How is Archie?"

"He misses you. Every day he asks where you are."

"I'm gonna talk to my landlord."

"Think it'll do any good?"

"No. But you've got to try."

"Offer them money."

"Like a bribe?"

"Oh, Ruzak. You offer to give them a deposit for any damage. That's usually how it's arranged."

"It probably would be better not to come to the table empty-handed. Thanks."

"I'm just looking out for Archie," she said. I could detect a smile in her voice. "She asked if you were wearing a hat."

"A hat?"

"I told her I couldn't remember."

"I've got one of those anonymous personas," I said. "I blend in."

"That must come in handy in your line of work."

"Well, I can't think of a single instance where it has."

She laughed for some reason. Some girls laugh only from the neck up. Amanda's laugh originated deep in her belly.

"Hey, you wanna hang with me sometime, Ruzak?"

"Now when you say hang? . . ."

"Maybe grab a cup of coffee. My treat. I know you're unemployed right now."

"Oh. Well." She wasn't my type, really, with that quasi-Goth look and the thinness. The dyed-black hair and that pin in her belly button.

"That's okay," she said without a hint of disappointment in her voice. "You probably have better things to do—like looking for your lost hat."

"No," I said. "Sounds terrific. I'd love to."

"I like you, Ruzak," she said. She still sounded amused. About my saying yes? About my desire for a dog? About my being nondescript? I wondered, given my intuitive understanding of the ineffableness of human beings, how I ever hoped to make a go at being a detective. It was like trying to use an electron microscope to look at a quark. Or maybe more like using one to measure the circumference of the sun.

NOVEMBER 20

NINE

*O*n the corner of the theologian's crowded credenza, next to the row of bobbleheads of Jesus, Moses, and Buddha, sat one of those four-cup brewers, and the professor offered me a cup from it after I sat down. The coffee slipped over the lip of the pot with the consistency of crude oil. He handed me the cup printed with a *Far Side* cartoon, the one with a big-headed kid in class raising his hand and saying, "May I be excused? My brain is full."

"I think I saw something in the paper about this case," Professor Heifitz said. He was a small man, pushing seventy, I guessed, with a bald, conical-shaped head, small, quick eyes, large ears, and an equally impressive nose. Our noses and ears never stop growing; I've never looked into what evolutionary purpose that serves, but I guess it has something to do with our fading senses. "But I don't recall any mention of the tetragrammaton."

"It might be one of those elements of the crime they hold back—in the event they identify a suspect."

"Have they?"

I shook my head. "I don't think they'd tell me if they did. I mean, it's not as if we have any kind of working relationship and, more importantly, I think I might be on their list."

"Ah. So that's it. You want to take yourself off their list."

"I'm sure that must be it. Self-preservation. I don't really have an alibi. I was alone that night."

"Rather like the victim himself."

"He wasn't alone. Somebody beat him to death."

"As I said."

"Ah," I said, thinking simultaneously that I was being infected by the academic miasma about me and of Eunice Shriver's book: *Ah! ejaculated Ruzak. I understand now.* "I guess there'd be nothing lonelier than that."

"It's an interesting bit of information," Professor Heifitz said. "The tetragrammaton is not what I would consider common knowledge."

"That's what I'm thinking," I said. "Along with hoping that the 'what' might help with the 'why,' which might lead to the 'who.'"

"Which led you to me."

"I thought about dressing up like a bum—or dressing down

like a bum, I guess—and hanging out at the railroad yards, but I've got that common fear of the homeless, plus the fact that I don't speak the lingo. They'd make me in two seconds."

He smiled without showing his teeth. Our teeth don't continue to grow past adolescence, but often that illusion is created as our face shrinks. He scooped a couple of dice from his desktop and commenced to rolling them in his hand. He played with those damn dice for the rest of our meeting.

"So what's the significance of the tetragrammaton?" I asked.

"I've no idea how it relates to this crime," he answered. "Obviously it holds some sort of significance to the killer, but I'm a theologian, not a psychologist, Mr. Ruzak."

"Right," I said. "I'll get with the Freudians later."

Again with the grin. "Perhaps you should start with the Jungians. All right. The tetragrammaton, as you already know, consists of four letters, rendered most commonly as *YHWH* but also as *JHVH, JHWH,* and *YHVH,* representing four consonants of the Hebrew alphabet: *yod, he, vav,* and *he.* Your Detective Black was correct when she told you the word is unpronounceable. The word, when it is rendered orally, is *Yahweh.*"

"The name of God?"

He nodded. "The name God gave himself in the burning bush. The tetragrammaton has been called 'the secret name of God' and appears often in the Dead Sea Scrolls and other ancient Hebrew literature. After the Exile in the sixth century B.C., the name fell out of favor, replaced more generally with the common noun,

Elohim. Interestingly, Yahweh is only one of these so-called 'secret names.' There were others. During the eleventh century, mystics known as *ba'al shem* claimed to work wonders and gain hidden knowledge by evoking the tetragrammaton and the other, more esoteric names of the Divine. The practice closely resembles certain shamanistic beliefs . . . that by knowing something's name one can master it or gain power over it."

"Gain power over God?"

"Or channel the power, to borrow a phrase from parapsychology. That would be more precise. By evoking God's hidden name, you gain a portion of his power."

"A power trip."

"Who has not, at some time or other, Mr. Ruzak, hungered for a taste of the Ultimate Ground of Being? To the ancient Hebrews, God is first and foremost the Creator, above and apart from his creation, inexpressible in language, and thus his name is rendered unpronounceable, a reflection of God's unknowable nature."

Not knowing what to say, I bought some time by raising the *Far Side* cup, allowing the lukewarm caffeinated sludge to touch my lips. *My brain is full.*

"Any of these—what'd you call them?—ba'al shems still running around ba'al shemming?"

"Not to my knowledge, no, but echoes of the practice remain in kabbalism and certain fundamentalist sects of the Christian church."

"And is that part of the practice, the writing on the forehead?"

He shook his head. "I've never heard of it."

"Does this seem plausible to you: You've got some disturbed individual with this fixation on at least two things, this tetragrammaton business or God in general and homeless people; and he feels he's been chosen to 'deliver' these lost souls back to God, sort of like a *Catcher in the Rye* syndrome only with old transients and not kids, or those hospice workers you read about who are offing the terminal patients right and left."

"Again, I'm not a forensic psychologist, Mr. Ruzak. But I will say mercy killings usually don't take the form of a savage beating. It is hard to imagine a more brutal way of 'saving' someone."

I thought of the stories of Job and the Crucifixion, but I didn't bring it up. I had no desire to go toe-to-toe with a theologian.

He looked at his watch. It swung loosely on his withered wrist when he lifted his arm. "Is there anything else, Mr. Ruzak? I'm late for class."

"Just one more thing," I said. "I was wondering . . . do you find it tough, your line of work? I mean, in these times is faith more like clinging on the edge of a cliff by your fingernails than taking up arms against a sea of troubles?"

"Clarify your question, Mr. Ruzak. Are you asking if faith is harder now than it was in the past?"

"I'm asking if we've finally gone too far and killed off God."

"Oh, I believe God is more resilient than that, Mr. Ruzak. He is more than happy to suffer us for a few more millennia."

TEN

*W*alter Newberry was a big man, a former Marine, semi-pro boxer and recovering alcoholic who found God literally while lying in a gutter on Magnolia Avenue. He came to at three in the morning, face-down, and when he pushed back from the concrete he saw the warning sign that read NO DUMPING/EMPTIES DIRECTLY INTO RIVER, with its picture of a fish. At that moment he heard Jesus calling him to begin his rescue mission, which he financed entirely through private donations.

"Saw this show on Discovery last Easter," I told him. "About how the early Christians traced a fish in the sand as a secret sign in Imperial Rome."

We were sitting in the mess hall of the mission house on Broadway, about five blocks from the spot where he fell ten years ago, landing on his stomach, which saved him from choking to death on his own vomit. Lunch was finished and the kitchen was already prepping for dinner. The mission was entering the busy season.

His massive head gave a nod. He was wearing a tight white T-shirt, blue jeans, and brown work boots. His right bicep sported a SEMPER FI tattoo.

"And early celebrations of the Last Supper always included fish," he said.

"That's one thing that struck me as a fat kid going to church," I said. "All the eating in the Bible, especially in the New Testament."

"And drinking. Look at all the metaphors Jesus used involving wine and vineyards. And his first miracle took place at a feast. He often referred to the Kingdom as a place of feasting."

"Way to a man's heart?"

"And his soul. What can I do for you, Mr. Ruzak?"

"Tell me about Cadillac Jack."

"Showed up about seven or eight months ago. Never said where he was from, but his accent was pure Yankee. Real quiet. Always came late for the meals, sat in the corner up there, near the door. I try to talk to all the folks who come in, but he was a tough nut to crack."

"So you didn't—crack him?"

He shrugged, staring over my shoulder at the plate-glass window facing Broadway.

"I will say this: Over sixty percent of the people who come through those doors have some kind of mental condition . . . borderline schizos, manic-depressives, you name it. Over ninety percent have a substance-abuse problem."

"Including Jack?"

He nodded. "Including Jack. And he was what I'd call . . . slow. You could tell in five minutes that the elevator didn't go all the way up, you understand what I mean?"

I told him I did. "Anything else? Anyone who had a beef with him?"

"Not that I know of. He always struck me as pretty harmless. Gentle. I remember one time, he came in with this stray cat . . . or kitten, I guess, that he found on the street somewhere. He was crazy about that cat, and I bent the rules a little for him. Let him bring it inside. Don't know whatever happened to that cat. Probably took off on him."

"Anybody around here he was especially close to, besides the cat?"

"Yeah. Guy named Jumper."

"Jumper?"

"Yeah. That's what they call him; never heard his real name. Haven't seen Jumper in a while, though, but that isn't unusual. He probably went south with the hummingbirds."

I asked him to describe Jumper. I scribbled down his description. Newberry watched me scribble.

"I already gave all this to that lady cop," he said.

"Well, it's not a competition."

"You gonna tell me your interest?"

"I was the one who found him."

"So?"

"So, well . . . have you ever been in the position where you've got nothing better to do and not doing something is sort of like embracing death?"

"Brother, now you're tugging at the knot."

"You ever hear of the tetragrammaton?"

"The tetra what?"

"Grammaton. The four-letter secret name of God."

"I always spell his name with three letters."

"Let me ask you this. You get any . . . oh, I don't know how else to put it, fanatics in here? Frothing-at-the-mouth religious types?"

"There's very few atheists in foxholes, Ruzak. It's all in your perspective. A fanatic to you might be a good Christian to me."

"No, I think this would be somebody a little more wild-eyed."

"You're welcome to come back at six. We get more preachers, proselytizers, and table pounders than you can shake a stick at."

I wrote my home number on one of my cards and asked him to call if he thought of anything else or if Jumper reappeared.

"You should come back," he said. "Work the serving line. Thanksgiving's coming up. We could always use an extra hand."

"I'll think about it."

"Do you know him, Ruzak?"

"Know who?"

"Jesus."

"We've never met."

"You're wrong about that, you know."

My face felt hot, the same reaction I had when Amanda asked me out.

"That's my conundrum," I confessed. "The knot I pull at. It's been my experience it just gets tighter."

NOVEMBER 27

ELEVEN

*W*hat's the matter with you, Ruzak?" Felicia asked as she wiped Tommy's mouth for the fifth time. "You look like crap."

"Crap!" Tommy barked.

"Don't say that word," Felicia told him. "It's not nice."

"But you said it, Mommy," Tommy said. The table jiggled as he swung his pudgy legs.

"I've been thinking seriously about picking up one of those light boxes," I said. Nature goes niggardly with light in late November. Midmorning could just as well be midafternoon, to judge by the light eking through the cloud cover. I slurped my coffee. This was my first time at the Market Square Diner, which had opened a couple of months after the former occupant, The Soup Kitchen, had cleared out. Felicia and I had lunched at The Soup Kitchen before it closed. I had been sorry to see it go. So sorry I'd refused to try this new place, as if to do so betrayed an old friendship.

"Seriously," she said. "What's up with you, Ruzak?"

"Ruzak!" shouted Tommy.

"Don't do that," Felicia scolded him, as if *Ruzak* was on par with *crap*.

My eyes strayed from her face. Through the window on my right, I could see the southwest corner of the square and the Suntrust Bank building, where in warmer months the crazy preacher man waved his pamphlets and exhorted the lunchtime crowd to dump Mammon for Jesus.

"Do you believe in God, Felicia?"

"This is important?"

I nodded. "Yeah. That's the bigger question. Is it really important anymore?"

"It's about that bum, isn't it?"

"Jack. His name was Jack Minor. They called him Cadillac."

"Why?"

"I haven't found out yet."

"You haven't . . . Ruzak, what have you been up to?"

"Just asking around, really."

"Asking who?"

"This professor of religion at UT. Guy who runs the mission on Broadway. And Thanksgiving I worked the line for a few hours."

"What line?"

"The food line at the mission."

"And you're doing this because? . . ."

I shrugged. Our food arrived. Tommy had the pancakes from the kids' menu. They were in the shape of a mouse's head, vaguely Disneyesque. A huge glob of butter perched precariously on top of the heap. Felicia spread it over the pancakes using her butter knife, eyes darting from my face to Tommy's plate.

"Let the cops handle it, Ruzak."

"I called them," I said. "Or her, actually. Detective Black. You know what she said? She asked if I knew how many homicides occur in the greater Knoxville area in a single month."

"How many?"

"I don't know. But the implication was they weren't going to bust their ass tracking down the killer of some anonymous transient."

"So that means you have to?"

"It's no big deal," I said. "And I'm not violating the court order or anything. I mean, nobody's paying me."

"And nobody's paying you to study for your exam, either. Time, like money, should be invested in something that has some kind of return, Ruzak."

My omelet was a little runny. I wiped up the yellow slop with the edge of my toast. I hated it when she lectured me, as if I were Tommy's big brother.

"And somebody *is* paying, Ruzak," she went on. "You look terrible. And you smell stale."

"Stale?"

"Stale, like you haven't changed your clothes in a week."

"Just my jeans. It doesn't make sense to wash denim after just one—"

"When's the last time you had a haircut?"

"I always let it grow in the winter," I said. "To conserve heat. Eighty percent of our body heat is lost—"

"Don't go over the edge on me, Ruzak."

"No. No, I'm at least fifty feet from the edge. Fifty to forty feet . . ."

"Seriously, why don't you pack up your study guides and hit the beach for a couple of weeks?"

"I was never a big fan of beaches. When you think about it, jumping in the open water is like running through the woods in your underwear. Plus I'm self-conscious about my body."

"Look around this restaurant, Ruzak. How many skinny people do you see?"

"Not as many as I saw on Thanksgiving."

"Oh, Ruzak. I'm gonna call 911: Your heart is bleeding."

"Families, Felicia, whole families . . ."

"Right; that's right, Teddy, and if you don't pass that exam, maybe next Thanksgiving you can join them on the other side of the steam table—you, me, and Tommy."

He looked at her at the sound of his name. Syrup hung from his bottom lip and dotted his chin. I pulled the napkin from my lap and ran it over the lower half of his wide face. He grinned at me. "Ruzak!" he shouted, and Felicia shushed him.

"I burned my thumb," I said, showing her the reddened pad. Half my print was gone. "On the steam. Made me think a determined killer could erase his prints that way."

"He'd be determined but not too bright."

"You read about them cutting off the fingers of their victims to hamper identification. They could just burn the prints off."

"I think they usually torch the whole body. Why are we talking about this over breakfast?" She glanced at Tommy, who was tracing designs in the puddle of syrup on his plate.

"So you do believe in God?" I asked again.

"I was raised to."

"But you don't now?"

"Frankly, Ruzak, I don't give it much thought."

"Whoever killed Cadillac did. I think he thought about it a lot." I told her about the tetragrammaton. "I thought it was just drawn on his forehead, Felicia, maybe with a piece of charcoal or even a Sharpie. But Detective Black told me it was *carved*. Somebody took some kind of sharp implement and cut it into his forehead. It looked dark to me that morning because of the frozen blood."

She glanced at Tommy, then leaned over the table and hissed sharply, "Ruzak, I'm not going to warn you again."

"Sorry. My point is, whoever did this thought it was very important to leave the secret name of God on his victim's forehead."

"Maybe Cadillac was a human sacrifice."

"And the killer puts God's name on him like a claim ticket?"

"Or like a parent writes their kid's name in their jacket."

"Right: 'Here, Yahweh, you left this down here; better pick it up.'"

"And that's where Teddy Ruzak, pseudo PI, comes in. Keeper of God's lost-and-found."

"You're saying I should drop this."

"Oh, yeah. Now you understand."

I picked up the check, since Felicia and Tommy came on my invitation. Felicia insisted on leaving the tip (as a former waitress, she never thought I tipped enough), and popped Tommy's hand when he tried to snatch the bills from the table.

On the sidewalk, she zipped his coat. The wind had picked up, and the clouds now looked like a sheet of corrugated steel above us. We walked south, away from the main square where the city sponsored free concerts in the summers. After we had walked about a block, Felicia leaned toward me, lowering her head slightly, and I could smell peaches.

"Don't turn around, but there's some old woman following us."

"Okay."

"She was in the restaurant, too."

"It's Eunice."

"Eunice who?"

"Shriver. No relation to the Yankee Shrivers. You remember her, the chronic confessor."

"Oh. Right. Why's she following you, Ruzak?"

"She's taken up a different kind of confessing."

Felicia gave me a look. I said, "She's writing a book about me."

"You're kidding."

"I can't figure out why, but she's been following me for a couple of weeks now. I've decided not to confront her. She's really old and working through some issues. They're issues I'd rather she work through alone."

Tommy ripped free from Felicia's grip and bulled his way between us, slipping his gloved paw into my right hand, taking Felicia's left with the other. A stranger might mistake us for a family.

"I wonder why you feel more kinship with the corpse in the alley than a living person who might need your help," Felicia said.

"What's wrong with Eunice Shriver I don't think I'm qualified to help."

"So what do you thinks qualifies you to help Cadillac Jack?"

"Sorry, I forgot. Teddy Ruzak, pseudo PI."

"You're sore."

"I haven't been getting much sleep," I admitted. "I can't get it out of my head, Felicia. I looked out that window and he's staring up at me, and from that height you can't tell . . . you can't tell if he's looking back or looking at nothing, and that's what's getting to me—the possibility that that's exactly what he's looking at: nothing; nothing at all."

TWELVE

I was taken aback at her car when, after she strapped Tommy into his car seat, Felicia turned and asked me if I wanted to come over for dinner.

"Now whose heart is bleeding?" I asked her. The wind drew a thick strand of her blond hair across the bridge of her small nose, and she pulled it away, tucking it behind her right ear. Suddenly I felt like bursting into tears.

"No way," she answered. "This is purely selfish. I've got to keep you healthy or it's back to the unemployment line."

"Actually, I guess you could say I sort of have this kind of date tonight."

"Really?" She reacted as if I had told her I had just crapped my pants, her nose crinkling the same way it did when she laughed. But she wasn't laughing.

"I'm having coffee with my pet consultant."

"You don't have a pet."

"That's what I'm consulting about."

"Seriously, who are you dating, Ruzak?"

"Nobody you'd know. She works at the pound."

"Oh. The philosopher."

She ducked her head a little, fumbling with the door handle of her Corolla. I was no mechanic, but the front tires looked a little bald to me, and I wondered how Bob, being a fireman and supposedly very up on safety issues, could let her drive around like that.

"She's prelaw," I said. "Which makes me suspect the philosophy thing is just a cover."

"A cover for what?"

"Rapacious greed."

She laughed. "Doesn't sound like your type, Ruzak."

I held the door for her as she slid in behind the wheel. She pulled down the visor and flipped open the mirror to check something in her reflection. I didn't know what she was checking. Tommy was yelling my name and Felicia told him to be quiet. I opened his door to say good-bye. He tugged on my wrist and ordered me to get in. Felicia told him to let go of Ruzak. As the car pulled away from the curb, the kid flattened his nose against the window. I raised my hand, then dropped it into my overcoat pocket before turning away.

I stopped at a vending machine to buy a paper. I doubted there'd be anything about Cadillac, but I had been checking every day, and why break the habit now? I tucked the newspaper under my arm, crossed the street into the little park, and sat on a bench beside Eunice Shriver. She was hiding behind her own copy of the *Sentinel*.

"So how's it going?" I asked.

She lowered the newspaper and said, "I have reached a crossroads."

"Best to take the one less traveled."

"That could be my life's epithet," she said.

"Epitaph," I corrected her. "Big difference."

"I have not wished to bother you, Theodore," she said. "Some battles we are doomed to fight alone."

"Right," I said. "Eunice, I saw you outside the mission. You shouldn't be hanging around down there. It's a terrific place to get mugged."

"You were there," she pointed out.

"But I've got about fifty pounds on you and I can affect a menacing air."

"Menacing, Theodore? You?"

"I've got facets you've never seen, Eunice."

"Yes! Facets! That's exactly what I'm after."

"What you're after," I echoed. "Eunice, I've been thinking about this little project, and the more I think about it, the more I'm convinced you've chosen the wrong subject. You're like a blind person trying to describe the color blue. Why don't you write *your* story? I'm sure it's much more interesting than mine."

"But Theodore, I can't drop it now; I'm nearly halfway done!"

"You're kidding."

"Look at my hands."

I looked at her hands. She said, "I've been having to wrap them at night in warm towels. The pain from typing all day becomes quite intense by eleven or twelve."

"Maybe you should dictate it."

"I thought of that, but I loathe the sound of my own voice."

"Most people do," I said. "Because the bones in our head distort the sound."

"Oh, my," she said. "My." She dug into her canvas tote and retrieved a pad and a pen. "'The bones in our head,'" she mumbled as she scribbled.

"So what's this crossroads you're talking about?" I asked.

"Theodore, I'm going to need much more involvement from your end."

"Eunice, from the beginning I think I've made it pretty clear I don't want any involvement, from any end."

"I need to get inside your head."

"That would make it about one person too crowded for me."

I had hurt her feelings. She lowered her head and studied her scuffed orthopedic shoes.

"Vernon tells me I'm foolish, too," she said softly. Vernon was her oldest child. I'd never met Vernon or any of her children, but I had the impression he was the one she was closest to. Maybe I should talk to Vernon, I decided, if you can make a decision that begins with the word *maybe*.

"Well," I sighed. "I guess if they had tied Michelangelo's hands behind his back, he would have painted the Sistine Chapel with his right foot. Tell me what you need, Eunice."

THIRTEEN

Amanda and I were sitting on the second floor of a coffee house in the southernmost building of the complex that fronted Kingston Pike, called Hamburg Place. The buildings next to the Pike had that sort of German, sort of Swedish look, with the fancy gables and dark trim, very Alpine-ish, though I wasn't sure if the Alps were even in Germany. Our table overlooked the parking lot. Railroad tracks lay on the other side of the lot, and on the opposite side of the tracks was the golf course. In warmer months, you parked by the tracks at your own risk.

She had clipped back her short, black hair using these wide, silver pins, the same kind my mother used to wear. Black parachute pants, a tight black T-shirt that revealed her pale torso and the silver pin in her belly button. She ordered a double espresso. I got something called the Turtle, a coffee concoction made with steamed milk and hot chocolate.

"So did you talk to your landlord?" she asked.

"How much time do I have?"

"Depends on how many we get in."

"I was wondering," I said. "About his name."

"I named him Archie."

"After the comic?"

"What comic?"

Despite being about ten miles from campus, the shop was crowded with students. Textbooks, laptops, highlighters, over-flowing ashtrays, chess sets. Floor-to-ceiling bookcases marched along the walls, with stacks of beat-up boxes of board games—Monopoly and Sorry and Risk—jammed between them.

"Maybe an old boyfriend?"

"He just looked like an Archie to me."

"That's good," I said. "I prefer human names for animals. Not like Fido or Stinky."

"Stinky?"

"My first—and only—dog was named Lady."

"Let me guess. Bulldog."

"Collie."

"At least you didn't name it Lassie."

"Lassie was a male."

"Not on the show."

"My dad named her. She died one summer when we were on vacation. I had a total meltdown. He told me I couldn't have another dog until I could demonstrate some self-control."

"And you couldn't?"

"Not to his satisfaction."

"You didn't get along?"

"I never saw him much. He was a salesman."

"The traveling kind?"

"The mediocre kind. He had to work very hard for the very little we had."

"I haven't spoken to my father in six years."

"Divorce?"

She nodded. She finished her espresso like a Russian sailor knocking back a shot of vodka.

"Parents," she said, and shuddered.

The guy sitting alone at the table behind her was typing on his computer, the white wires from his iPod dangling from his ears. He was smirking, maybe at something he was listening to or reading, an e-mail or MySpace comment, and I said, "Did you hear about that study that found Americans have only about two close friends?"

"No."

"It struck me how disconnected everything is, though we're more connected now than in any time in human history."

"Do you really think about things like that?"

"Three hundred million of us and growing, yet we're lonelier than ever."

"Maybe you're projecting."

"That's the thing. I don't want to get a dog simply because I'm lonely."

"Isn't that the best reason to get one?"

"I think it has more to do with my savior complex."

"Oh, God. Not one of those."

"I was a kid," I said. "I thought that damn dog died because I wasn't there to save her. I thought if only I had been there . . ." Something caught in my throat. You never really stop grieving. It just goes into hiding, like a filovirus into the dark recesses of the rain forest.

She reached across the table and placed her hand over mine. Her fingers were ice-cold.

"I like you, Ruzak," she said. "You got heart."

"A hemophilic one."

"There are worse kinds."

I walked with her across the parking lot. I watched our breath congeal into mist and mingle.

"Sit in the car with me a minute," she said.

Her car was a late-model Monte Carlo. She cranked the engine to get the heat going, then threw herself over the seat at me, wrapping those pale, thin arms around my neck and smashing her lips into mine. Her tongue was insistent against my front teeth. I could taste the acidity of her espresso. Her cold fingers dug into the hair on the back of my head.

When she came up for air, she said, "You know what I think your problem is, Ruzak? You're a little in love with death."

She grabbed my right wrist and lifted my arm, pushing my hand under her black T-shirt. I was struck by the contrast between the warmth of her chest and the coldness of her fingers.

"Don't tell me you're gay," she whispered.

"I'm not," I said.

"Kiss me again, Ruzak. Hard."

I kissed her again, my arm twisted awkwardly between us. I worried about my two-day-old beard, if it was irritating her soft skin. It seemed strange to me, her accusing me of being in love with death when she was the one in black; I'd never seen her wear a different color.

She broke the kiss and I removed my hand from beneath her shirt. She glanced in the rearview mirror and then unsnapped her pants and commenced to wiggle out of them.

"What's going on?" I asked.

"Tell me you're a virgin. Please." Her cheeks were flushed. The foggy window behind her shone with the ambient light of the single streetlamp about two cars away.

She pushed me back against the seat and straddled me. Her panties were white. I was surprised.

"Come on, Ruzak," she whispered into my ear. "I haven't been laid in months."

It had been much longer than that for me, but I didn't tell her that. Her hips rotated slowly as her weight pressed down on my lap, with both hands on my shoulders, pushing.

"Don't you like me?" she asked. "I can tell you like me. . . ."

"I do like you," I said. "I do."

"But? There's a 'but' there."

I bit back an inappropriate laugh. "This is just a little . . . sudden."

"Spontaneous." Again she smashed her lips against mine. There was nothing tender about it. Insistent and fierce, bordering on angry.

When I could talk again, I said, "I can't shake the feeling I'm taking advantage of you."

She pushed herself off me and sat behind the steering wheel again, taking it in both hands, like a little girl pretending to drive her daddy's car.

"Sorry," I said. "I've been edgy ever since I found him."

"Who?"

"The old guy in the alley."

"See? You are in love with death."

"I really don't see it that way, Amanda."

"Then why won't you fuck me?"

I didn't say anything. She swung her face in my direction.

"I turn you on," she said. "I felt it."

"Do you believe in God?"

"Huh?"

I repeated the question. She said, "Oh great, one of those. This is just my shitty luck." She hit the steering wheel with the heel of her hand.

"So that means you don't?"

"No, I don't, if you must know."

"The evidence could be interpreted either way."

"Who cares, Ruzak? Who really cares anymore?"

She grabbed her pants from the floorboard and yanked them over her slender hips. "I like you, Ruzak, I really do, but guess what? You haven't been commissioned to save anybody. You may think you're preserving my honor or whatever, but really, all you're doing is leaving me frustrated and fucking angry and thinking I'm unattractive as hell. . . ."

I reached over to wipe off the tear rolling down her cheek. She slapped my hand away.

"Don't fucking touch me."

"Sorry. You're not. It's me. You know it's me."

"I don't want to get engaged or have a boyfriend and, even if I did, it wouldn't be with someone like you," she said. "I don't need a man to complete me. And guess what, I don't need God or Jesus or any of that other bullshit. It's all bullshit, Ruzak. Even love is bullshit. You know what love is? Love is just a complex hormonal response to stimuli. It's genetic memory mixed with the procreative drive. It's the lie we tell our children because the truth is too horrible to say aloud. You're thinking love saves but love does the opposite. Why are you looking at me like that? Who are you, Mahatma Fucking Gandhi?"

"I was just thinking this has got to be the oddest first date I've ever had."

"Fuck you."

"Amanda . . ."

"Get out of my car and fuck you."

"Okay."

I stepped out but left the door open. I leaned in.

"I'll call you," I said.

"Don't you fucking dare."

She started the car and slammed it into reverse before I could close the door. I stepped back in the nick of time. She floored the gas. She stopped long enough to reach over and shut the door, and then she was gone, screeching out of the parking lot. I suspected she was hyped on caffeine, which can be as dangerous as driving drunk.

I sat in my car for a minute or two, and then dug my cell phone from my pocket. Felicia answered on the fifth ring.

"Hey," I said.

"Ruzak?"

"Hope it's not a bad time," I said, checking my watch. I figured Tommy would be in bed.

"What's the matter?" Felicia asked. "I thought you were on a date."

"It's over."

"Something bad happened, didn't it?"

"I've got to get out of this funk," I said. "I was thinking finding who killed that old guy might get me out of it, but now I'm wondering if that's just making it worse."

"Of course it's making it worse."

"I took his mug shot to the soup kitchen," I told her. "The one taken when he was busted for B and E. I showed it to everyone who came by my station. Nobody remembered him. Nobody knew he had even been there. They didn't know the face. They didn't recognize the name. He passed through life as anonymously as a boat in the fog. Do you think I have a complex?"

"Oh, Ruzak, don't get me started. You made some ham-handed pass at her, didn't you, and got your face slapped."

"No, just my hand."

She didn't say anything.

"Are you still there?" I asked.

"Yes."

"Okay. I thought the network had dropped my call."

"You want me to come over?" she asked.

"I'm in my car."

"Well, I could wait till you get home, dummy."

"No," I said. "No. You have Tommy."

"Bob can watch him."

"Bob won't mind if you come over?"

"We're all grownups, Ruzak."

"That's okay. I think I'd rather be alone. Sorry to call."

"Ruzak, drop this."

"I will. I mean, I should."

"And it's a good idea for you to talk to somebody. You know, a professional. Something's going on with you and I'm not qualified to deal with it."

NOVEMBER 30

FOURTEEN

I brought some lilies for my mother's grave and a bottle of Old Grouse for Dad's. Mom had buried him among the Baptists, though Dad had never set foot in a Baptist church, or any church for that matter, since his twenties. He had asked to be cremated and his ashes scattered over the Smoky Mountains. Mom claimed to have looked into it before telling him federal law prohibited dumping a person's remains in a national park.

"Well, Mom," I told her. "I got to get to the printer's, but I wanted to let you know I'm not a detective anymore. Actually, I guess I never was, but anyway, despite that or maybe because of that, now I'm looking into this case of a guy I found dead in the alley behind my office. Nobody asked me to and Felicia tells me not to; she says it's dangerous to my mental health, but I can't get it out of my head, him lying down there in the garbage, like he was looking up right at me, and I can't get it out of my head that the last thing he saw was the person who killed him, and I'm wondering if he was still alive when they carved those letters into his forehead, though the coroner doesn't think so because there wasn't much blood and there'd be more if his heart was still beating. He had seventy-three broken bones, Mom. He was a mess. Face, ribs, arms, fingers, both cheeks. They beat the living shit out of him. Sorry.

"Damn, it's cold. I prefer February cold to November cold. November cold seeps right in and you can't shake it, even in a warm room.

"So anyway, I'm supposed to be studying for the PI exam so I can do this the right way instead of the Ruzak way, but you know, part of this I'm convinced must be genetic; Dad was a corner-cutter, let's be honest. Remember how he lost that job in Saint Louis, skimming commissions from his crew at the car dealership? Or how he used to park in the handicapped spaces at the grocery? Dad thought the fix was in on everything, even elections and pro football games, so he never saw anything wrong in putting the fix in himself. I'm not being judgmental, Mom. It's not judgmental to face the facts.

"I know what you'd tell me. You'd tell me to pray about all this, and I've tried but I can't get past 'Dear God.' I start and then my mind gets overwhelmed and my thoughts scatter and I feel this weight come down on my shoulders like it's too much, and I feel like a kid poking a big anthill with a stick. That's weird. Then I think most people in my position would choose to escape or anesthetize themselves, which is just another form of escape, I guess. Like the vast majority of homeless people are alcoholics and a big chunk are also mentally handicapped, and this Cadillac Jack was both, but I've checked with every mental institution, hospital, and drug rehab clinic in eastern Tennessee, and nobody has a record of ever treating a Jack Minor.

"The ways to catch a killer are finite, Mom. Forensics, witnesses, victimology, profiling . . . maybe one or two more, but that's about it. I guess I keep looking at Jack because he was looking at me. Maybe to catch his killer I need to look away. Like with God, you're not going to find him by looking for him.

"So that's why I got to stop by the printer's on my way home."

I unscrewed the cap of the Grouse and slowly poured the whiskey over Dad's grave, near the base of the stone, aiming for the spot directly over his mouth. Then I dropped the bottle back into the bag and slipped it into the outer pocket of my overcoat.

"It's the last day of November," I said. "Thank God."

A man was standing on the handicap ramp leading to the side door of the church, watching me as I walked back to my car. He raised his hand and I waved back. I stood by the car for a second, and then decided, What the hell? I crossed the lot and stood on the pavement beneath him while he leaned his forearms on the rail, smiling benevolently down at me with large, perfectly even teeth.

"How are you, Eddy?" he asked.

"It's Teddy, and I'm a little cold," I told Pastor Morris. He was wearing a gray suit and a bright yellow tie with a silver cross tiepin. His goldish-blond hair was swept straight back from his finely sculpted forehead. Pastor Morris was at least six years younger than I was, a fact that made me vaguely uneasy for some reason.

"Want to come inside for a minute?"

"I'm late for an appointment," I lied.

"How's business?" he asked.

"Not bad," I lied again.

"Working through your weekends?"

"As a matter of fact . . ." I said, but stopped there. Let the preacher fill in the blanks; that was sort of his job.

"We surely miss your mother," he said, nodding toward the cemetery. "She was a wonderful woman."

"You think it borders on the profane, my talking to her grave like that?" I had to assume he had seen me out there.

"In what way?"

"Well, you know, talking to the dead, like some sort of ancestor worship."

"Talking isn't the same as praying, Eddy."

"Teddy."

"Just closing your eyes and feeling God's presence—that can be praying, too."

"I caught this documentary on TV not long ago," I said. "About that tsunami in Indonesia. This one Indian guy was with his family on a train, heading for a holiday on the coast, when it rolled in and he never found his son, this twelve-year-old kid. He was just wiped off the face of the earth."

"So what's your point?"

"Well, he never talked about his religion, but I'm betting he said a prayer."

"The Almighty has his own purposes."

"That's the rub, Pastor. Why did he give us a brain if he didn't want us to figure out what those are?"

"Are you asking me why we suffer?"

"No. Because I know what your answer's going to be. Original sin or free will or echoing Christ's suffering or something along those lines. I just can't shake this feeling that God was born on the day the first person died."

I sat for a few minutes in the car. The forecast was calling for the first snow of the season. The preacher disappeared into the church. He was barely three months on the job when he buried my mother, and he kept getting her name wrong at the service. Maybe it didn't make much difference in the eternal scheme of things, but I was pretty upset at the time. The ancient Hebrews invested a lot of time and energy ferreting out the hidden name of God, and not just because God was important to them; *names* were important. I wouldn't be the same person if my name had been Ralph or Anthony or Christopher—or even Eddy, which this preacher obviously thought it should be.

By forgetting her name, he was forgetting her, and the point of the whole exercise was to remember.

FIFTEEN

*A*manda laid down her paperback copy of Nietzsche's *Man and Superman* when I walked through the glass doors.

"This better be about Archie," she said.

"That's half of it," I said. "Well, a third."

"You don't owe me an apology, Ruzak. What do you have behind your back? Those better not be flowers."

"If it is, am I in trouble?"

"Oh, Christ. They'll just die. I'm here till four and I don't have anything to put them in. What are they?"

I showed her.

"Daisies?"

"It was more of an impulse buy," I said. "I was at the florist's picking up some lilies for my mom's grave."

She grabbed the flowers and laid them behind the counter.

"The second thing," I said, to move off the subject of flowers. "I was wondering if you'd mind putting this on the door."

I showed her one of the flyers I'd been putting up all over town.

"Who's Jack Minor?" she asked.

"The old guy who died behind my building."

"Twenty-five-thousand-dollar reward? Who's putting that up?" She looked at me.

"I collected a pretty big payoff on my first case," I explained.

She stared at me for a few seconds more, then shrugged and dropped the flyer beside the daisies.

"I'll ask the boss."

"The third thing," I said. I took a deep breath. "I've decided to adopt Archie."

"You can't."

"Because I'm underqualified?"

"Because he's dead."

"Oh, no."

"They put him down this morning, Ruzak."

"Why didn't you call me?"

"I did call you. I left a long message on your voice mail."

"I wasn't home. I was visiting my mom."

"I thought your mom was dead."

"I was visiting my dead mom."

"Well, Archie joined the club at ten-forty-five this morning."

"Well, of course he did."

"What's that supposed to mean?"

"I have to go," I said.

"Don't do that. Three more came in last night. Let's check them out."

"No," I said. "No. I still have to cover Cumberland Avenue."

"Carpe diem, Ruzak!" she called after me as I walked to the door. "Carpe diem!"

I sat in my Sentra and put my hands on the wheel. I wondered if she could see me. Bits of snow began to peck at the windshield, no bigger than pencil leads, not soft, fluffy-looking flakes, but flinty pellets, a vindictive snow. The prospect daunted me, trudging up that long slope on Cumberland Avenue in this weather, stapling my "Wanted" posters on the light poles along the section known as The Strip, the main drag through campus. In a day or two, Jack's face would be buried under other announcements and advertisements more interesting to college students, local band dates and roommate-wanted flyers with the little removable strips with the contact information at the bottom.

Covered over. Busted up. Jack was pulp inside, his gut filled with blood, both lungs crushed. The only significant exterior bleeding had been from his forehead, and that was after his heart had stopped. Jack Minor bled into himself; they turned him into a sack of blood and shattered bone, then cut the name of God in a spot no more than an inch from the only part of his brain that had the capacity to conceive of a God.

The cops had found a broken piece of two-by-four near the mouth of the alley, which Meredith Black thought was a good candidate for the murder weapon. The crime techs had found several human hairs that resembled Jack's stuck in one splintered end, but they had no plans to run a comparison. What would be the point of that? Detective Black had six other homicide cases on her desk demanding her attention, cases with leads and tips and real evidence to work from. No witnesses had come forward, and nobody had walked through the front doors of the station to confess. She had a better case with the gang-banger from the East Side who took a bullet in the forehead. He didn't have much of a future, either, but there were people who noticed his passing, for whom each day was different because he died.

Behind a closed door, one person holds down the animal while another injects it with a lethal dose of pentobarbital. The animal is dead in thirty seconds. Then they place it in an oven and burn it. Three to four million times every year. And it's okay; it's the humane thing. Nobody wants this dog. The man holding the needle is performing a necessary service to society. We can't allow these creatures to run wild on the streets. They're a nuisance and a burden.

SIXTEEN

I arrived at my apartment a little after five, in a darkness that struck me as preternatural. There was no message from Amanda. Felicia had left a message to call her.

"I haven't heard from you in a couple days," she said.

"Well," I said. "No news is good news."

"Ruzak, you're not having a nervous breakdown, are you?"

"You know what I think it is? That Hinton guy from the state left the cosmic door open that day he shut us down and some seriously bad karma blew into the room. They killed Archie today."

"Who's Archie?"

"The dog I was going to adopt."

"Oh. Who killed him?"

"The people my tax money pays to kill them."

"Ruzak, I know you've got your heart set on it, but maybe a dog isn't the right kind of pet for you. Maybe you should go with something that doesn't require quite that level of commitment."

"What, like a turtle?"

"Or a hamster, if it's got to be a mammal. What about a parrot?"

"Parrots aren't mammals, and I read somewhere they can live to be a hundred. I'm not comfortable with having a pet that will outlive me."

She changed the subject. "You'll never guess who called me today. Eunice Shriver."

"Why'd she do that?"

"To talk about you. She's a funky old broad. She kept me on the phone for two hours."

"I'll talk to her. People with obsessive personalities should have the decency to keep it to themselves. What did she want to know?"

"It was weird. She kept talking about you as if you were hypothetical."

"What's that mean?"

"Oh, she'd say things like, 'If this guy you barely knew walked into the diner where you were working and offered to give you a job, bing, just like that, what would you say?'"

"Well, that's pretty much what happened."

"Or, 'Say you had this thirty-something bachelor with limited social skills, let's call him Teddy, how do you think he'd approach you, as a woman? . . . '"

"She wonders if I'd approach you if I was a woman?"

"*Me* as a woman, Ruzak. *Me*."

"Oh. What did you say?"

"I said I would let him know I was involved in a relationship."

"I've been meaning to call Vernon."

"Who the hell is Vernon?"

"Her son. I'm thinking an intervention might be necessary."

"I think she's harmless. Aren't you flattered?"

"More like unnerved. Her grip on reality is one-handed."

"Right now I'm more concerned with *your* grip," Felicia said. "Have you been studying for your exam?"

"I've been kind of busy."

"Doing what?"

"Looking for my hat."

"Oh, Ruzak."

"Look, I should tell you in case you see them around somewhere: I've made up these posters offering a reward for Jack's killer. Well, not a reward for his killer, but one for information leading to the arrest and conviction of his killer."

There was a second or two of silence, and then she said, "What kind of reward?"

"The monetary kind."

"Christ, Ruzak . . ."

"Only twenty-five thousand."

"Oh, is that all? Ruzak, you're talking to someone who happens to know the balance in your account."

"It's okay," I said. "It's okay. I'm not dipping deep, not up to my neck, just sticking a toe in."

"More like going up to your waist."

"Well, we could quibble."

"You'll have fakes and con men coming out of the woodwork, Ruzak. Anybody with any legitimate knowledge is going to take it to the cops."

"I don't have to pay out unless there's an arrest and conviction. By that time I'll have passed the test and be back in business. And that's all I'm gonna do, Felicia; I promise. No more sleuthing until I have my license. I think he'll be happy with that."

"You think who will be happy?"

"Jack."

"Ruzak, Jack is dead."

"I know. That's how this whole thing started."

"You remember Dr. Fredericks?" she asked.

The shrink. Something knotted up in my chest. I said, lips tight, "Sure I remember her."

"Maybe you oughta give her a call."

"You bet."

I was chilled to the bone, so I took a hot shower, wrapped myself in a towel, and fried some bacon for a BLT in the cast-iron skillet I'd inherited from Mom. Halfway through the frying, the towel slipped from my middle and puddled around my ankles. It's not a good idea in general to fry anything in the nude, but some masochistic switch had been flipped in my psyche, and the hot grease popping on my pale flesh brought me a kind of perverse satisfaction. I thought of those pilgrims who flagellate themselves on their way to shrines, though the odds weren't in my favor that I was on some march to enlightenment. The odds were more likely I was slipping down a slope toward a messy landing. The evidence was there, like Eunice Shriver asking Felicia questions that implied my existence was merely hypothetical. The evidence was there that both Eunice and I had climbed into the same metaphysical boat, and that boat was being carried by a swift current toward the falls.

DECEMBER 4

SEVENTEEN

I signed in at the front desk, and the cop behind the counter gave me a visitor's pass to clip on my shirt pocket. Then I followed a short young woman, whose uniform struck me as at least two sizes too small for her, through a set of double doors, and down a series of labyrinthine hallways until we reached a door outfitted with one of those keypad-locking systems. The door was labeled HOMICIDE. She blocked my view of the keypad with her body as she punched in the code.

"Last office on the right," she instructed me.

Detective Meredith Black smiled at the sight of me filling her doorway.

"How've you been, Mr. Ruzak?" she asked. She reached across the desk, gave my hand two quick pumps, and waved me to a chair. On the credenza behind her were several photos of her with two kids, a boy and a girl, neither more than ten, I'd guess. No man in any of them. Divorced, probably, or maybe he took all the photos. Or they could be a relative's kids.

I could have filled her in on the details of my escalating existential crisis, but I had been pegged for a kook by law enforcement during my first case, and I was determined this time to present a sturdier façade.

"Thanks for seeing me," I told Detective Black. "I know you must have your fair share of wannabes and hangers-on and rubberneckers."

She smiled enigmatically. I wondered why I had made a list like that. Just doing it up thrust me into the milieu.

"Well, I really don't have that much to share with you, Mr. Ruzak. As I told you on the phone, the case has stalled."

"Don't know if you've seen or heard about this," I said, sliding the poster across her desk. "And I owe you an apology, I guess, for slapping them up all over town without giving you a heads-up. I have this tendency to go off half-cocked."

"Seems counterproductive in your line of work, Mr. Ruzak."

"Oh, practically every personality trait I have is," I said. She was studying the poster. "So I tell myself it's like my old shop class: Sometimes you have to saw against the grain to get the perfect cut."

"It's an admirable gesture," she said, dropping the poster on her blotter.

"Meaning futile?"

She shrugged. "I haven't gotten any calls. You?"

"A couple. Nothing promising."

"Well, then."

She leaned back in her chair and folded her hands in her lap. She wore a gray cashmere or cashmere-looking turtleneck sweater and gray slacks. I noted the prominence of her chin. The chin and those large incisors, that's what Meredith Black led with.

"I've got a couple a working theories I'd like to run by you, if that's okay," I said. She didn't say it was, but on the other hand she didn't say it wasn't, so I went on. "Nothing past the hypothetical stage. There are things I know but more things I don't know, and some of the things I don't know you may know. That's what I need to know, so I know which to keep and which to toss."

"Which what to keep or toss?"

"Theories. For example, what do you know about Jumper?"

"Jumper?"

"According to Walter Newberry, Jumper was Cadillac's only friend in Knoxville. He disappeared near the time Jack was murdered."

"I interviewed Mr. Newberry. I don't remember him mentioning any Jumper."

"Well, he mentioned him to me. So I'm thinking we're dealing with either a suspect or a witness."

"There's a third possibility. It's a coincidence. Jumper's disappearance has nothing to do with the crime."

"Right. So you don't have anything on Jumper?"

She shook her head. "As I said, Mr. Ruzak, this is the first I've heard of him."

"Okay. Well, he isn't really necessary for my working theories to work. He's the best candidate I have for Theory A, but it could be someone else, a Mr. X. By the way, I'm calling the perpetrator in Theory A 'Mr. X,' and in Theory B he's 'Mr. Y.'"

"A, B, X, Y, got it," she said.

"Okay, so . . . Theory A: Jack Minor was murdered by somebody he knew. First, he was beaten to death, an intimate way to kill, right up there with stabbing. Mr. X knew Jack and had some motivation to kill him. Mr. X could be Jumper or another person Jack knew in town. Maybe Jack stole something from him, or Mr. X demanded money from him, or Jack welshed on a bet . . . it could be any number of things."

She was nodding. "Agreed."

"Whether premeditated or spur-of-the-moment, the beating probably occurred where I found him. There's a possibility he died someplace else and the body dumped in the alley, but that would entail some risk for Mr. X. If Jack was indebted in some way to him, I figure Mr. X lured Jack to the crime scene on a pretext, then jumped him."

"I'm beginning to see how someone named Jumper could fit into this scenario."

I took a deep breath. "It's also possible within the paradigm of

Theory A that Jack was the instigator—in other words, Jack set up somebody to rob them and lost the fight."

"In that case, Mr. X doesn't have to be someone he knew. I'm assuming Theory B has to do with a stranger killing."

"Right. Mr. Y is a complete stranger, a psychopath with a God complex who knocks off Jack for his own disturbed reasons—that's what behind YHWH. He may have been stalking Jack or other transients, or maybe Jack was a victim of opportunity. . . . Mr. Y sees him that night and lures or follows him into the alley."

"Or perhaps Mr. Y is someone Jack knows."

"That would make him Mr. X."

"My point is, that segment of society is full of people with psychological and emotional problems. It isn't farfetched that Jack knew someone obsessed with religion, and this person decided to make an offering out of him."

"Which is why it seems imperative to me we try to find this Jumper. He might be the key. The one thing Mr. X and Mr. Y have in common is YHWH. Plus the fact that Jumper is the only real lead we have."

"Mr. Ruzak," she said, and her tone was not unkind, "As I've said, the department takes every homicide very seriously, and simply because this homicide involved an indigent doesn't mean we take it any less seriously than someone murdered in, say, West Knoxville. But I hope you can understand we simply don't have the manpower to track down every possible lead in every single case. This case has no witnesses, no promising forensics, and no viable suspects, X, Y, or Z."

"My theories didn't have a Z. You think there could be a Z? A Z would imply a C when I thought A and B covered every possible scenario using X and Y."

She showed me her incisors, chin thrust slightly forward. "Here's one possible C. Jack was murdered by a secret society or cult that worshiped the ancient Hebrew god Yahweh. Either as a ritual sacrifice or because he saw something he shouldn't have seen or stole something he shouldn't have stolen. Like a sacred amulet or code belonging to the cult. Maybe you should look into all the functioning secret death cults in the county. Then, after you nab them, sell the film rights to Hollywood. You could call it *The Yahweh Code*."

I thought about what she just said. "You think this is funny."

"I think it's pitiful. Not you—Jack. Well, maybe you a little, too." She tapped her well-manicured index finger on the poster. "Don't get me wrong, Mr. Ruzak. Offering a reward is really altruistic and noble, and I promise if any calls come in on it, you'll be notified. As I hope you'll notify us should you develop any leads."

"I have developed a lead and I did bring it to you," I said. "Which you poo-pooed."

"You said it yourself: that's not a lead; that's a theory."

"It's both."

She shrugged. "I can make a few calls about this Jumper

person, but I'm assuming you've already done the legwork and come up empty, otherwise you wouldn't be here asking about him."

"I don't believe you," I said. "I don't believe you'll make a single call and I don't believe you take this case as seriously as you would a rich person buying it in West Knoxville. I don't think you care jack squat about Jack Minor. He was a nobody—not anything to anyone except God, if you believe in a God, and maybe that's why whoever did this carved those letters into his forehead, like a return address. And just like Jesus being taken up in a cloud, Jack is gone from our sight, but the ironic thing, he was gone before he left."

I stood up. "And I'm going to find whoever did this, Detective Black. I'm going to find him and deliver him to your doorstep, because you've made it clear I'm all Jack has now. Me, of all people! The most hapless PI to come down the pike since Inspector Clouseau, that's who Jack Minor has on his side."

"The Pink Panther wasn't a PI, Mr. Ruzak," she pointed out, smiling.

"Well, the plain fact is I couldn't think of any famous PIs who are also hapless. Hapless PIs are invisible, too."

EIGHTEEN

*L*ater that afternoon, I was on my daily phone call with Eunice Shriver when another call beeped through. I told Eunice I would call her back because I never could get the hang of clicking the button to put people on hold; I always disconnected them. So I held down the button and picked up on the first ring.

"Good, you're home."

"Amanda?"

"What's your number?"

"You just called it."

"Your apartment number, Ruzak. I'm outside your building."

"I'll come down."

Amanda was sitting on the front stoop, cradling something

squirming in a fleece blanket. Being an ace detective, I immediately deduced what it was.

"That's a dog," I said.

"Ruzak, it's Archie."

She pulled back the edge of the blanket and I saw dark brown eyes and a wriggling black nose.

"You told me they put Archie down."

"I know. I lied. Can we go inside? He's freezing."

"Let me make sure the coast is clear."

We took the stairs to the third floor; the elevator was too risky. I threw the deadbolt and Archie leaped out of Amanda's arms as if that was the signal he'd been waiting for. He scampered through every room, skittering on the hardwood, and once he had run the circuit, sniffing along the baseboards and in the corners, he came to a stop in front of me and sat, his tail scraping back and forth as he grinned up at me.

"I think he approves," Amanda said.

"My landlord won't."

"What your landlord doesn't know won't hurt him."

"I'll have to take him for walks," I said. "Sooner or later they'll catch me. That's the thing most transgressors never figure out, Amanda: Eventually, everything in shadow comes into the light."

"That sounds like something from the Bible."

Well, you can bet it didn't come from your pal Nietzsche, I thought. "Why did you lie to me?"

"I was angry. You hurt me and I wanted to hurt you."

"I was that cruel?" It seemed to me the punishment didn't fit the crime.

"Ruzak, you and me disagree on most of the fundamentals, but I think we both can agree that I'm human. Can you think of anything crueler than rejection?"

"Yes. Indifference."

"You're going to reject Archie now, aren't you? Just to get back at me."

I looked down at the dog. His eyes were the color of chocolate and fixed on mine. I'd learned from Animal Planet that you never look away from a dog's gaze; it was a sign of submissiveness. Dogs view humans as two-legged members of the pack, and you had to establish you were top dog. After a few seconds, Archie gave up trying to stare me down and fell to his side, raising his foreleg and offering his belly for a rub. I looked at Amanda.

"He's housebroken, right?"

"He never messed in his pen," she said.

"Guess I gotta get to the pet store," I said.

"I'll come with you."

"Will he bark while we're gone?"

"We'll take him with us. How about it, Arch? Wanna go shopping?"

So that's what we did: piled into my little Sentra and drove to Pet Market on Kingston Pike. Archie rode in Amanda's lap, and she insisted we keep the window down so he could stick his busy nose into the frigid air.

"Dogs have a sense of smell a thousand times more sensitive than ours," she pointed out.

I wondered if that applied to your flat-faced breeds, like bulldogs and pugs.

"What do you want from me, Ruzak? I'm just a volunteer, not a vet."

She was being awfully snippy for someone trying to right a wrong.

"What made you change your mind?" I asked.

"Today was Archie's day. They were coming at five to put him down. So I signed all the papers and paid the fees. You owe me a hundred and thirty dollars, Ruzak."

Pet Market promised the lowest prices in town, but after bowls, food, treats, a crate and bed, collar and leash, an ID tag with Archie's name and my phone number, a chewy toy, a package of dried pigs' ears, doggie shampoo, a comb, and a toothbrush, the total bill came to $312.87. I had no idea they made toothbrushes for dogs.

"What do you think?" I asked Amanda on the drive back. "Is getting a dog like purchasing friendship?"

"What, like buying something that can't be bought?"

"I've always looked at therapy that way. What does a shrink do that your favorite bartender can't?"

"Dispense drugs."

"Alcohol is a drug. And unless you've got a real problem, you can get out of a 'session' for a lot less than a hundred fifty an hour."

She helped me carry Archie's supplies up to my apartment. I set up his crate by the sofa and asked Amanda why I needed to cage this dog.

"A dog crate isn't cruel, Ruzak," she answered. "It gives them a sense of security at night and when you're gone. Dogs can develop separation anxiety. Crates help with that."

I offered her something to drink. I didn't think she deserved a reward for lying to me, but probably deserved one for rescuing Archie and forcing me into the decision I'd been avoiding for reasons I couldn't put my finger on. She accepted a beer and we sat on the sofa while Archie worked on his new squeaky toy, a lamb whose cries I guess excited the part of Archie's brain that still held the ancient memory of the hunt, the death squeals of the kill.

"Everybody has a type," she said. "People they're more attracted to than others. Is that it? I'm not your type?"

"I never really thought about it."

"What is that? Is that a yes or a no?"

"It's neither."

"Look, Ruzak, I'm young but I'm not stupid. You're not gay so I know you must look at women. What kind of women do you like to look at? You a leg man? Breasts? Ass? What?"

"Eyes."

"Eyes?"

I nodded and took a long pull of my Bud Light.

"What color are my eyes, Ruzak?"

"Brown."

"You guessed that because most people have brown eyes. They're green."

"I could have sworn they were brown."

"I don't have large tits. But my legs are okay."

"I've never seen them."

"It's winter, Ruzak. But I hardly ever wear skirts. Is that it, I'm not feminine enough?"

"Oh no. You're feminine."

"No I'm not. Not like my sister. I was always a tomboy; she's the girly-girl. Maybe you'd like my sister better."

"You want to set me up with your sister?"

"I'm just trying to figure you out. I'm attracted to you. I've never been attracted to a big guy before. You're really not my type. I like athletic guys; you know, guys with a nice build. But the biggest thing for me is intelligence."

I wasn't sure, but I thought she had just called me fat and stupid.

"That's a puzzle, then," I said. "Why you would find me attractive."

"I've had dreams about you."

"You're kidding."

"It's the size thing. You're so big and I'm skinny and in my dreams you're holding me down. . . . It's almost like a rape."

"Boy."

"And I'll wake up and, God, I'll be so excited."

She set her empty bottle on my coffee table and scooted closer to me.

"So what do you think?"

"My dreams are usually more mundane," I said. "Me in the kitchen trying to open a can of tuna fish. Things like that."

She put her pale hand on my knee and said, "It's just sex, Ruzak. I don't even expect it to be good sex, if you've got any issues with performance anxiety. We don't have to go steady or get engaged or anything like that. I'm on the pill."

My immediate instinct was to tell her I had AIDS. Then I thought that might be a little over the top and herpes would be better. I could tell her I was in the middle of an outbreak. Her eyes *were* green, but a very dark, loamy green.

"There's somebody else," I blurted out.

She stared at me for a second. "Where?" she asked, and then looked around the room as if the other woman might leap out from a hiding place.

"We've been dating for almost a year," I said.

She pulled away from me and said, "You might have told me before I admitted to having sex dreams about you. What's your goal, Ruzak? Why is it, every time I see you, you humiliate me?"

She grabbed her coat from the back of the sofa and stood up. Archie rose when she did and followed her to the door. It had been a big day for Archie, and Amanda was the one constant.

"I don't believe you, by the way," she said at the door. "You don't have a girlfriend. What's the big deal, Ruzak? Why can't you just tell me you find me gross?"

"I don't find you gross."

"Then what is it? You a monk or something? Are you on a mission from God, Ruzak?"

"This old guy has raised some questions in my mind. I guess they've been simmering on the back burner for some time now," I said, "And there's this principle I try to live by: When you're tumbling down a slippery slope, you don't grab onto anyone. You'll just yank them down with you."

"But what if grabbing onto someone is your only hope?"

I didn't have an answer for that. I thanked her again for saving Archie and she left. Archie pressed his nose against the jamb and whined, his tail waving slowly.

"She's gone," I told him. "And I doubt she'll be back."

A couple hours later, I realized I'd forgotten to give her a check for the adoption fee.

NINETEEN

*T*hat night the Discovery Channel ran a special about the ascent of man and the mysterious disappearance of the Neanderthal. Did disease or competition with us wipe them out, or did we murder them into extinction? In the nineteenth century, the Romantics viewed Nature as benign, a glowing reflection of God's grace. Now we know better. Nature is brutal and, if it is feminine, she's not the kind of woman you can trust. Human beings may be her finest achievement yet, but when you get right down to brass tacks, we're meat. AIDS and organisms like streptococcus don't give a crap that we subdued the earth or produced a Shakespeare or put a man on the moon or were the first species to conceive of God. We might not have been the first, though. Maybe Neanderthals got to God first. If true, that raises all sorts of theological issues I didn't feel qualified to deal with.

Two things disturbed my viewing pleasure. One was the dog. While I sprawled on the sofa, he lay on the floor by the television, head between his forepaws, staring at me. It started to get to me after a while. I asked him what he wanted. I offered him a Milk Bone, then a pig's ear. During a commercial, I rushed him outside for a quick walk, during which there was much sniffing but little urinating and no defecation. I worried he might be saving up for a deposit on my hardwood, and I remembered I'd forgotten to pick up some poopie-cleaning product at the pet store.

Back upstairs, he resumed his position by the TV, so it was impossible for me to ignore his stare while I tried to watch Cro-Magnon make his great migration. Maybe this was part of the separation anxiety Amanda had talked about.

"I'm not going anywhere," I told him. He answered with not so much as a twitch of his tail.

A little after ten the phone rang. Archie got up before I did. He followed me into the kitchen and stood there, staring up at me, still as a setter on point.

"Hello?" I said into the receiver. Silence. I glanced at the caller-ID display. It said, UNKNOWN CALLER.

"I'm on the do-not-call list," I said, thinking I was queued up in a phone bank. Silence. "Hello?" I said again. The line went dead.

Ruzak back to the sofa. Archie back to the TV. A commercial was on, the one with the two cavemen pissed off at the big insurance company. The phone rang again. Again Archie followed me into the kitchen. I glanced at the caller ID. UNKNOWN CALLER.

"Hello?"

More silence, but this time I thought I could hear someone breathing.

"This is Teddy Ruzak," I said. "Who's this?"

No answer.

"Amanda?" I asked. "Eunice?"

The line clicked, and then I heard the dial tone. I went to the bedroom; Archie's nails clicked on the hardwood as he followed me. I grabbed the cordless phone from its cradle and was halfway back to the sofa when the phone rang again.

I hit the talk button and said, "Look, I don't know who you are or why you're calling, but I'm in the middle of something important right now and the FCC considers what you're doing a serious crime. It's called harassment, and blocking your number won't stop them from finding out who you are."

Silence. I stood by the sofa. Archie sat at my feet.

"I can hear you breathing," I said. My mind raced down the list of the people who might call me. The list was short, and everyone on it wouldn't hold on the line without saying anything. I figured, if this wasn't some random weirdo, that I actually had a lead on the line. "Are you calling about the reward?"

They hung up. I waited for the phone to ring again. I was sure they would call back.

They didn't. Not that night, at least.

DECEMBER 5

TWENTY

I woke fully clothed on the sofa to the ringing of the telephone. I rolled over and the cordless fell off my stomach onto the floor. Archie was sitting by the coffee table about three feet away, watching me.

"Hello?" I gasped.

"Theodore, you never called me back."

"Eunice? What time is it?"

"Four-thirty."

"In the morning?"

"Old people never sleep; didn't you know that?"

"What's the matter?" I asked, because something had to be for her to call me at four-thirty in the morning.

"We haven't finished, and I do my best work in the morning."

"Really, Eunice, I'm not in good shape right now."

"Why, Theodore?"

"It's four-thirty in the morning!"

"I am beginning to sense a certain reluctance on your part to help me with the last worthwhile endeavor of my life."

"Well, I hope it isn't the last thing you do. That would be a helluva coda, Eunice. Did you call me last night, around ten-forty-five?"

"Now Theodore, wouldn't we both know if I had?"

"Somebody called three or four times and just held the line."

I heard a strange clicking through the earpiece.

"Did you hear that?" I asked. "Something just clicked on the line."

"That may have been my teeth."

"Your teeth?"

"My uppers slipped."

"Eunice, you're not taping me, are you?"

"Theodore, what a question!"

It could be a tap. But who would tap my phone? Archie had not budged since I woke up. Mouth slightly open, bright brown eyes locked on my face, he looked like he was grinning.

"I'm going to hang up now, Eunice," I said. "My dog needs to go outside."

"Dog? Theodore, you don't own a dog."

"I do now."

"Hmm. I'll have to think about the wisdom of using that device."

"Device?"

"The device of using a dog to create sympathy for the character."

"He's not a device, Eunice; he's a dog. And I'm not a character; I'm a human being."

She didn't say anything. I heard another click. I knew from my PI test material that taping someone without their knowledge was legal in Tennessee, but phone taps required a court order. Knowing that didn't kill the little germ of paranoia beginning to replicate itself in my sleep-deprived brain. I told Eunice again that my dog had to go wee-wee and hung up. I didn't get up from the sofa, though. Just sat there and looked at Archie looking at me and waited for her to call back.

"Do you need to go?" I asked him. He didn't move a muscle. Not even a twitch of his tail. Why was this creature staring at me? I've heard dogs are especially sensitive to stimuli that flies under our human radar, things like earthquakes and low pressure systems. Maybe Archie was picking up on something wrong with me, an imminent heart attack or aneurysm.

I scooped him off the floor and put him into the crate behind the sofa. He stared at me through the bars.

"Don't look at me like that," I said. "This is supposed to comfort you."

I threw myself on the sofa and tried to go back to sleep. I couldn't shake the feeling that I was losing my grip on something very important, not my sanity, per se, but my grip upon the familiar, the comfortable world I held so casually until the day Mr. Hinton walked into my office and yanked it out of my hands. Or was it that morning when I looked out my window and saw the dead man looking back at me, God's name emblazoned above his empty stare? I felt as if I had crossed a border into a new country, an immigrant who couldn't speak the language, my vocabulary useless in the Land of the Enigmatic Stare, where Jack Minor and Archie were natives. The string theory had unnerved me, but now I could see the seductiveness of it. In another reality, Teddy Ruzak had his detective license, Archie a house in the suburbs with a big yard and kids to play with, and even Jack Minor a place of his own where the sun shone more than ten days in the winter.

I gave up on sleep. On my way to the kitchen, I glanced toward the cage, and that dog was still sitting there, watching me. I let him out.

"What's the matter with us, Arch?" I asked. I made a mental note to call the vet as soon as the sun came up. There was something wrong with this dog. He couldn't tell me, but maybe a vet could.

"Come on, I'll fry us some bacon."

TWENTY·ONE

*W*hen the phone rang a little after ten, I checked the caller ID before answering. It said CITY OF KNOXVILLE.

"Mr. Ruzak," Detective Black said. "How are you?"

"Look," I said. "About yesterday. I guess I overreacted a little."

"Perfectly understandable. I hope I haven't caught you at an inconvenient time."

"Oh, no. All my time is convenient now."

She gave a little laugh, and I thought of those large incisors.

"I made some inquiries after you left, and I think I have a name for you."

Nincompoop would be a good one, I thought, but I said, "A name?"

"Jumper's real name is Reginald Matthews. He's been arrested three or four times on nuisance and reckless endangerment charges. They call him Jumper because he has a penchant for threatening to jump off various rooftops around town. He climbs up and waits for us to get there and talk him down."

"He's suicidal?"

"He may be, but usually when people really want to kill themselves they do."

She told me they had an address for him in Johnson City. I wrote it down.

"He listed his next of kin as Robert Matthews, his son, same address."

"Phone number?"

"Nope, and there's no listing for either of them. I checked."

"I guess you're not taking a drive up to Johnson City."

"Maybe I'm trying to save you twenty-five thousand dollars."

"Hey," I said. "I really appreciate this."

"Just doing my part to aid and abet an unlicensed PI."

I called the Humane Society and learned Amanda wouldn't be in till three. She probably had morning classes. I dialed Felicia's number. She answered on the sixth ring with a voice thick with sleep.

"I woke you," I said. "Sorry."

"I was up late with Tommy," she said. "He had a rough night."

"He's not the only one."

"What's the crisis du jour, Ruzak?"

"I've got to drive up to Johnson City and I wanted to know—"

"I can't go with you."

"I was actually needing a pet-sitter. Thought maybe Tommy would like to meet Archie."

"You finally got a dog."

"Or he got me; it's complicated."

"Why are you going to Johnson City?"

"I've got a lead."

"You've got a—is this about the dead bum?"

"Jack. Jack Minor. Yeah. There may be a potential witness or possible suspect up there."

"Tell the cops."

"Actually, the cops told me."

"Why would the cops tell you?"

"I guess I kind of shamed them into it. I wouldn't bother you, but I hate the thought of locking him up all day, plus I don't know how long this might take. I might have to stay overnight, depending on what I find. Do you mind watching Archie for me?"

"Is this animal housebroken?"

"Well, he hasn't relieved himself in my apartment yet."

"I'm worried about you, Ruzak. I can't figure if this whole thing is you working *on* something or working *through* something."

"Maybe a little of both."

Ten minutes later, I stepped out of the shower to find Archie sitting in the bathroom doorway, watching. I quickly wrapped a towel around my middle; I wasn't accustomed to another set of eyes seeing me naked. Archie had abandonment issues, I decided. That's why he stared, because if he looked away I might be gone.

"I'm not going anywhere," I told his reflection in the mirror while I shaved. "Well, actually, I am going somewhere, but I won't be long and you'll be staying with a very nice lady who has a kid that'll just eat you up."

He didn't react to the sound of my voice. I tried to remember if he'd wagged his tail since Amanda left.

"You ignored your breakfast," I went on. "I gave you a forty-five-minute walk. You don't want your squeaky lamb or a bone. What do you want, Archie? You keep watching me like you want something—what is it? What do you want?"

I turned away from the sink and squatted on the linoleum. I snapped my fingers. Archie stayed in the doorway, ducking his head a little, nose twitching, the tip of his pink tongue protruding between his brown lips.

"Come here, boy. Come on, Archie." I whistled softly. Archie didn't move. "Maybe you've been beaten," I said. "Maybe I even look a little like the guy who beat you and you're wondering why Amanda delivered you back into the hands of the enemy. I'll ask her if there was any evidence of abuse when they brought you in. It's okay, Arch, swear to God, you can trust me."

I stood up and took a step toward him. He got up and took a step back.

"I won't hurt you," I said. He turned and trotted down the hall, nails clicking on the hardwood, turning the corner and disappearing into the family room. Only no family lived here. What did you call the family room of a single person? I hung in the bathroom doorway, chewing on my lower lip. Something was going on with this dog. Maybe that's why his owner abandoned him. Who'd want a dog that stared at you all the time?

Felicia lived in a neighborhood just off Chapman Highway, on the southern edge of Knoxville, a few miles from the town of Seymour. It was only a twenty-minute drive from my apartment, but it seemed much longer with Archie sitting in the bucket seat beside me, staring at my profile. I was so distracted I almost rear-ended a Buick at the stoplight for the entrance to Baptist Hospital. My mom had died in Baptist Hospital, which sat on a bluff overlooking the Tennessee River. During the deathwatch, I would sit in the chair beside the window and stare outside at the opaque water sliding under the Henley Street Bridge.

At the door, Tommy pushed against his mother's legs, trying to get to Archie, hollering, "Puppy, puppy, puppy, I wanna see the puppy!" I set him down just inside the door and those two were all over each other, swapping slobber, Archie's tail a blur of white and brown, until the kid fell laughing onto his back and the dog jumped on his chest, swabbing the decks with his tongue. Felicia gave me a look.

"What?" I asked.

"Now, what do you think is going to happen when Buster has to leave?"

"His name is Archie."

"He looks more like a Buster."

"I didn't name him."

"Curse of the foster parent."

"He doesn't wag his tail for me," I said.

"He's going to eat the legs off my coffee table, isn't he?"

"I don't know what he'll do, to tell the truth," I said, watching Tommy and Archie frolic at our feet. "All he's done with me is stare. Here's his stuff."

"Just set it there by the door."

"Bob around?"

"No. Why?"

"Just wondering. You think I'll ever meet Bob?"

"Anything's possible."

"You'd think I would have by now."

"Do you want to meet him?"

"It's like we're Superman and Clark Kent: never in the same room together."

"Which one would you say is Superman?"

"That's funny, Lois."

"You sure about this trip, Ruzak?" she asked.

I nodded. "There's a reason Jumper took off right around the time Jack got killed. I find Jumper, I find the reason. I find the reason, I maybe find the killer."

"You sound like Charlie Chan."

"I'm a human being, Felicia."

"Wasn't Charlie?"

"I mean, I'm not a fictional character."

"Who said you were a fictional character?"

"Nobody, but somebody implied it pretty strongly around four-thirty this morning."

"Oh, Ruzak, a guest at forty-thirty? Who was it, that Amanda person?"

"Eunice Shriver."

She cocked her head to one side and her nose crinkled.

"It was on the phone, Felicia," I said. "Okay, I better hit the road. Archie, come here, boy."

Archie ignored me. He had a grip on Tommy's wrist and was play-growling deep in his throat. Tommy was laughing so hard that tears streamed down his face.

"Archie," I said. "Come say good-bye to Daddy."

"Daddy?" Felicia asked.

"All right," I said. "That's okay. He's made a friend."

I turned on the stoop to say good-bye, but the door was already closing. I saw Tommy on the floor, Archie squirming in his pudgy arms and Felicia fussing at both of them. Then she threw the deadbolt.

TWENTY-TWO

Johnson City, named for the seventeenth president, was situated in the far northeast corner of Tennessee, about one hundred miles north and a thousand feet higher than Knoxville, in an area alternately called the Tri-Cities (the other two being Bristol and Kingsport) and the "state of Franklin." During the Civil War, this portion of the state seceded from the Confederacy and petitioned the Union to be admitted as a state, following the model of West Virginia. Johnson City, like Knoxville, was a college town, home to East Tennessee State University.

It had snowed over the weekend, the snow followed by a cold front that plunged the temperature into the teens. The hills encircling the city glistened pure white, but the snow piled beside the road and in the parking lots was that dirty-orange color that reminded me of deli mustard.

Holiday banners festooned the lampposts along State of Franklin Road, and the cars of Christmas shoppers packed the mall parking lot. This would be my first Christmas without family. Dad had a couple of brothers living in upstate New York, but I wasn't close to my uncles. Dad had trouble getting along with family, though he never met a stranger he didn't like.

I was thinking about that as I pulled into a space near the food court entrance to the mall: The focus of the season is family, but the thrust of Christmas, the point of the whole damn thing, is the stranger and the outcast, the anonymous losers living among us. Mary and Joseph bunked with animals in a barn and Jesus, who was God on earth after all, spent his first night in a food trough. When I was a teenager and the absurdity of this first hit me, I made the mistake of telling my mother, who was offended down to her Baptist shoestrings. I was convinced that we were worshipping a deity crazy as a bedbug and, if he was, what did that make us? She rewarded me with a slap across my mouth. Atheists and their fellow travelers point to Islamic terrorism as a wake-up call that we'd better abandon God or the biblical disasters attributed to him will pale in comparison to what we'll end up doing to ourselves. In other words, God may not be dead, but keeping him alive endangers the human race.

I wondered if Jack's killer was getting at something along

those lines with the tetragrammaton. Maybe he wasn't a religious fanatic at all. Maybe he was a psychotic atheist, though more people have justified their crimes by citing their love of God. In our time, the devil is out as the scapegoat. They say the 9/11 hijackers screamed "God is great!" right before they murdered three thousand people.

According to the Knoxville PD, Robert Matthews lived only a few blocks from the mall, but I had decided on the drive up not to attempt contact till later in the day. Odds were he'd be at work and I might get only one shot at this, since he might be harboring a fugitive. Plus, it was now after one o'clock and I was starving.

I ate at the Ruby Tuesday in the mall, then returned to my car and located the apartment complex where Robert lived or might live. I parked a couple of buildings away from his unit and commenced my surveillance. Gas was pushing three dollars per gallon, so I cut the engine and buttoned my coat up to my neck. Within an hour, I fell asleep.

TWENTY-THREE

$\mathcal{D}$usk was creeping in from the east when I woke up a couple hours later. It was so cold my nose had gone completely numb. I stepped out of the car and stamped my feet on the frozen pavement, and the sound of it was very loud in the frigid air. I was feeling a little spongy; there was no other word for it.

Robert Matthews lived in apartment 213 in Building C, and I trudged up the stairs to the second floor, unbuttoning my coat as I ascended: I didn't want to be mistaken for a pervert, which I associated with men in buttoned-up overcoats.

I rapped on the door. I blew hard into my cupped hands. My knuckles had turned bright red. What if I had died of hypothermia in the Sentra? How long before somebody found me? It was a persistent worry since I moved from my parents' house, that I would die alone in my apartment, and days would pass before somebody noticed I was missing. Now I had a dog, and what would that animal do if his owner fell over from a massive coronary or aneurysm and couldn't put out the Alpo for a week? The thought was too terrible to contemplate.

The door opened and a woman in her late thirties, maybe, eyed me standing on the welcome mat.

"I'm looking for Robert Matthews," I said.

"He's not here."

"But this is his address?"

"Who wants to know?"

"Teddy Ruzak."

"Who's Teddy Ruzak?"

"Me. I'm Teddy Ruzak. I'm a PI out of Knoxville and I'm trying to find his father."

"His father doesn't live here."

Behind her, I could see a toddler with half his fist in his mouth, naked but for a diaper, his knees the color of charcoal.

"When will Robert be home?" I asked.

"Who is it, Liz?" a man called from inside.

Liz rolled her eyes and called over shoulder, "Somebody looking for Reggie!" She gave me the once-over and said, "He just got home."

"Who?" He appeared behind her, wearing a grease-stained pair of overalls with his name stitched on the right breast: ROBERT.

"Teddy Ruzak," I said. "How's it going?"

He ignored the question. "Are you a cop?"

"He's a PI," Liz said.

"Technically, I'm an investigative consultant."

"What the hell does that mean?" Robert asked. He had a small, pinched face, reminding me of those mammals that emerged from their primordial holes after the dinosaurs bit the dust.

"Basically it's a reflection of the age we live in," I said. "I'm a specialist."

"What do you want with Reggie?"

"I think he might be involved in a murder."

"Murder! You got some kind of ID or something?"

I handed my business card to him through the half-open door.

"'Highly Effective,'" he read. "That what you are, highly effective?"

"Well, there's good days and there's bad days."

He stared at me for a long moment. His wife was staring at him, and the toddler was staring at her. I stared at nothing and tried to look trustworthy.

"All right," he finally said.

"Robert," Liz said.

"It's okay," he assured her, and I followed them into the small family room with a sofa that had seen better days, worn carpeting, and cheap plastic vertical blinds over the sliding glass doors leading to the patio, where Fisher Price and Mattel were staging a major invasion. The kid, whose name I never caught, stared at me, gnawing on his knuckles, a dab of something the color of peanut butter on his knobby elbow. Robert offered for Liz to fetch me a beer. I thanked him, but I was still feeling a little spongy and asked instead for a cup of coffee. Liz left to brew some.

"Now, what's this about Reggie?" he asked.

I gave him one of my flyers.

"Twenty-five thousand dollars," Robert murmured. He studied the picture. "This isn't Reggie," he said.

"No. It's a man named Jack Minor. He was found murdered in an alley last month. Actually, *I* found him murdered in an alley last month."

"There ain't no way Reggie murdered anybody," Robert said.

"Reggie ever mentioned Jack Minor to you? He may have used the name Cadillac."

"I haven't spoken to my father in eight years."

"Is there a reason for that?"

"Oh, no. No reason. Just been real busy. Jesus Christ! What do you know about Reggie Matthews, Ruzak?"

"I know he's been in and out of treatment centers, been arrested more than a couple of times, and likes the view from tall buildings. Down in Knoxville he's called Jumper, though that's a misnomer since I don't think he's actually ever jumped. And the most significant thing I know is your dad vanished around the same time his friend Jack Minor was murdered."

Liz came in the room with a cup of coffee for me and a Miller Lite for Robert. She planted herself on the settee by the television. The kid picked up a stuffed bear and waddled over to me, holding it out.

"He wants you to hold it," Liz said. I thanked him and pulled the bear into my lap. It was missing an arm, and the white stuffing bulged from the tear. There was something disturbing about that.

"Reggie ran out on me and my mom when I was twelve. Very seldom I'd get a postcard or a phone call, then about eight years ago he completely disappeared. I just thought he drank himself to death."

"You didn't know he was in Knoxville?"

"I didn't know where the hell he was and I didn't care. He was nothing to me."

The little boy, emboldened by the big man with the red nose accepting his gift, commenced to bringing me other toys he scooped up from the floor, until I had a lapful.

"Okay, buddy, enough of that," Liz told him, but he ignored her.

"What about other relatives? Brothers, sisters, cousins?"

"Nobody," Robert said. "Nobody at all."

"Why did he leave Johnson City?"

"He was never in Johnson City, far as I know. Me and Liz moved up here last year."

"That's odd," I said. "Last time they arrested your dad, he listed this apartment as his address."

His eyes narrowed over the neck of his bottle, and Robert said, "So?"

"So if you haven't seen or heard from him in eight years . . ."

The kid, having relocated all the toys in the room to my lap, hoofed it down the hallway and disappeared into another room. Liz didn't notice; she was watching Robert.

"He probably just gave them my name as the next of kin and they looked it up," he said with a shrug.

Their boy returned with a toy rifle longer than he was and, face split wide with giggles, offered it to me. Liz fussed at him but I said it was okay, and leaned the rifle against the arm of the sofa. The kid barked a laugh and raced back down the hall.

"Was your dad very religious?" I asked.

"Was he what?"

"There's a theological component to the crime," I said. "Whoever killed Jack had some kind of obsession with God."

"The only thing that obsessed Reggie was Jack Daniels."

"How about you?"

"You think I didn't learn my lesson? I never touch hard liquor." He tucked his empty bottle between his thighs. His knuckles were encrusted with grease. If I were Liz, I wouldn't let him near the furniture until he had showered and changed out of the grungy overalls.

"No, I meant how do you feel about God?"

"What is this? Are you a PI or a Jehovah's Witness, Ruzak?"

"Neither."

"Then why the hell are you here?"

"Well, that's a good question and something I've been wrestling with. I'm a big guy, but no matter how big you are, there are some questions that'll always be bigger. My gut tells me Reggie didn't kill Jack Minor, but he may know who did and that's why he took off. He's afraid he's next. So my theory is—to answer your question—my theory is, given your classic fight-or-flight response, Reggie has 'gone to ground,' to a place where he feels safe."

"He wouldn't be safe here," Robert said. "I hate that sonofabitch's guts."

At that moment, his son reappeared, head, eyes, nose and cheeks hidden under my next present, fat little arms outstretched, stumbling along a little bowlegged toward me, until he bumped into the sofa and fell back on his diapered butt. Liz rose from the settee and moved toward him as he yanked the floppy brown hat from his round head and waved it toward me.

"Sorry," Liz said to me.

"It's okay," I said, taking my hat from the child squirming in her arms.

"Nice hat," I said.

TWENTY-FOUR

I drove to the lot on behind Robert Matthews's apartment and parked on the backside of Building C. There was a six-foot space with a walkway between the buildings, so I could see the base of the stairs leading down from Unit 213. Night had fallen, and the temperature could not have been much over twenty degrees. A hard freeze was coming.

I called Felicia's number and got her voice mail. I hung up without leaving a message. Ten minutes later, my phone rang.

"Where are you?" she asked.

"Sitting in my car. Hey, listen. I'm gonna be a little later getting back than I expected."

"How much later?"

"An hour. Or a day. It depends."

"On what?"

I told her. She asked, "Are you sure it's your hat?"

"There's a stain on the brim," I said. "Mustard from a hotdog I had at Sonic. It's my hat."

"Do they know they're busted?"

"I didn't confront them about it, though maybe my reaction to the mustard stain gave me away. I don't know; I'm not much of an actor."

"He did it. Jumper. There's no other reason to hide him."

"Unless they're protecting him from the killer."

"Nope."

"Why nope?"

"Twenty-five thousand reasons why nope, Ruzak."

"For all they know I'm the killer—that was my line of thinking."

"And the reward is the bait to lure the witness from his hole?"

"Right."

"Hmmm. Robby doesn't sound that sophisticated."

"He's a mechanic."

"So?"

"So mechanics intuitively understand the principle of interlocking, moving parts. Anyway, I figured they needed time alone to debate the pros and cons of coming clean with me."

"So what's your plan?"

"Wait awhile for the call. I figure it'll be sooner rather than later. How's Archie?"

"He's watching TV with Tommy. They've exhausted each other."

"Any unnatural staring?"

"No, just the natural kind. Why?"

"I'm starting to think it's something about me and not the dog."

"The odds are better. Oh, and Eunice Shriver called again."

"Why?"

"Because you won't give her your cell phone number and I really wish you would. I would have, but she hung up before I had a chance."

"She hung up on you?"

"She was pretty pissed she couldn't get hold of you. This is none of my business, Ruzak, but I don't think that old woman is quite right in the head. She threatened to cut me out."

"Cut you out?"

"Of the story. Well, her exact words were, 'I'll be forced to red-pencil you.'"

"Have you ever heard of the string theory?"

"No, but I get the feeling you have, and now you don't have anything better to do than to tell me."

"Boiled down to its nub, basically there are an infinite number of possible existences, and everything that could possibly happen *does* happen in one of these, um, alternate realities."

"Wow. What's that have to do with string?"

"Maybe reality is like a rope, which is made up of thousands of tiny individual strands of fiber or strings, each one having its own integrity but part of the larger intertwining."

"Intertwining?"

"Right. So maybe in this rope there's a string where I *am* a fictional character."

"And another string where you're not?"

"The question is, Which string am I in?"

"It seems pretty far out there, Ruzak. The possibility that you're the product of an eighty-six-year-old woman's imagination."

"It's lost some of its luster in the scientific community," I admitted. "And even if it were true, what can I do about it?"

"Beg her to let you win the lottery."

"A lot of money would be nice, but I'd rather have the answer."

"The answer to what?"

"Oh, you know, what's it for. If there's a purpose. If the unconnectedness is an illusion and God really does have a plan."

Above me, in the moonless sky, the stars shone winter-bright in the dark matter—the stuff that made up 98 percent of the universe, the stuff that scientists had so much trouble understanding, which meant we couldn't grasp 98 percent of the reality surrounding us.

"Ruzak, are you there?"

"I guess I am. I hope so," I said. "Felicia, do you think I should have slept with Amanda?"

She didn't say anything at first. "Does it matter what I think?"

"I mean, I'm not talking about the carnal act per se, though it's been some time since I—"

"Ruzak, I'm really not comfortable talking about this."

"I don't mean her personally, that's the thing. And not the sex part, but the idea that we're only afforded a finite number of opportunities to . . . to . . . to . . ."

"Connect with someone?"

"Or forget that we can't. That ultimately, because of the dark matter that separates us, we can't."

"You've lost me, Ruzak. Look, you need to walk away from this. You need to drive back to Knoxville right now, and in the morning you can give the police what you know and let them handle it. It's their job, Ruzak. Your job is to study for the PI test, because it's next month, and if you flunk that test I'll never forgive you. Do you hear me? I will never forgive you, Ruzak."

"I gotta go," I said.

"Teddy—"

"Somebody's calling through," I said. "I'll call you right back."

"Mr. Ruzak," Liz Matthews said after I picked up. "I hope you're not too far down the road."

"Not too far," I said.

"I have a confession to make."

"So do I. I'm not down the road. I'll be up in two minutes."

TWENTY-FIVE

*R*obert had showered and changed into a pair of jeans and an ETSU sweatshirt. He occupied the lounger in one corner, the flyer crumpled in his hand. With the fingers of the other, he nervously combed his damp hair. Maybe they put the kid to bed or locked him in his room, I didn't know, but he wasn't around to bring me any more presents. Liz was sitting on the sofa next to her father-in-law, Reginald "Jumper" Matthews, thin-faced like his son, white-haired, splotchy-skinned and shrunken-looking in a denim shirt two sizes too big for him. I guess the shirt belonged to Robert. And the baggy jeans. And the athletic socks on his jittery feet.

"Is this for real?" Robert asked, waving the flyer in my direction.

"It's for real," I said. "And if Reggie helps us nab this guy, he gets every penny."

"You hear that, Dad?" Liz asked. Reggie nodded. She turned to me. "You understand, Mr. Ruzak, we wanted to clear all this with Reggie first."

"You bet," I said. "What did you see, Reggie?"

"Hold on," Robert said. "Maybe we need to talk about it first. How do we know you won't take this information and keep the money? Maybe we should talk about some kind of up-front money."

"That's not the offer," I said. "The reward hinges on the arrest and conviction of the killer."

"Look, Ruzak, a couple weeks ago my old man shows up at my door scared shitless. Look at him—he's still scared shitless. Me, I'm thinking he's gone out of his head again with the booze or God knows what else, saying they're comin' for him next, and to-day you show at my door looking for him, and what am I sup-posed to think but maybe he's right, maybe somebody is after his ass. So I gotta think after his safety, you know what I mean? I gotta look out for Reggie. If this is on the up-and-up, I don't see how a little earnest money's gonna hurt. Maybe ten percent down, fully refundable if the information doesn't pan out."

"I'd be okay with that," I said. "If we put the money in some kind of escrow account."

Robert's eyes narrowed. "What, you don't trust me?"

"Looks like there's a lack of that on both sides."

"Not me," Reggie spoke up for the first time. "I trust you." He looked at Robert. "He's got a good face."

"Christ, Pop," Robert said.

"I don't understand why you're offering it in the first place," Liz said to me. "Who put up this reward money?"

"If you're asking who hired me to find Jack's killer, nobody did. The money is mine."

"So why, Ruzak?" Robert asked. "Who's Jack to you?"

"Nobody—except I'm the one who found him, and that's the issue."

"You're like the Good Samaritan, huh?"

"Well, as I remember the story, the guy he helped actually lived to tell the tale."

I looked at Reggie. "We don't need to complicate this. Reggie gets the cash when I get the killer."

"And when you screw up and the crazy mothers come after my dad, then what? You cover the funeral expense?"

"Well," I said, trying to puzzle it out—I had no idea how I'd stumbled into such a complicated negotiation. "Maybe we can set up some kind of protection program along the lines of the FBI—"

"And who foots the bill for that? We got him back into treatment, but my insurance don't pay for that or his Prozac, and who's gonna pay for his upkeep until these bastards go to trial?"

"Robert," Liz said. "We had this problem before Mr. Ruzak showed up."

"It's Reggie's information," I said, hunting for the shears to cut the Gordian knot. "Maybe it should be Reggie's decision."

Everyone looked at Reggie. He didn't say anything. Robert finally said, softly, "Reggie ain't been capable of making a decision for twenty years."

"You're my boy, and listen at the way you talk to me," Reggie said. "Maybe I just won't tell nothin' to nobody."

He crossed his arms over his thin chest and stuck out his grizzled chin defiantly toward Robert.

"Here's what I'm willing to do," I said. "Half the reward deposited in an interest-bearing account in Reggie's name, plus half his living expenses until we get this guy behind bars."

"You don't need to worry about that," Reggie said, "because I ain't no charity case. I'm leavin' tonight."

"Right, Pops," Robert said. "That's what I'm workin' on here." He turned to me. "Deal, but you're protecting him henceforth and henceforward, Ruzak. Understand? I got a wife and little kid to think about."

We shook hands on it, and Liz asked if I wanted another cup of coffee. I accepted, hoping the caffeine would suppress the gnawing hunger in my belly: I hadn't eaten anything since lunch at the mall. She went into the kitchen. Reggie called after her, asking her to fetch him a glass of ice water.

"One thing first," Reggie said to me. "I ain't goin' back to Knoxville."

"I don't see how we can avoid that," I said.

"They said they would kill me if they ever saw me again."

"Who?"

He looked away. His hands worried with each other in his lap. The knuckles were oversized, or maybe he just had thin fingers. Liz returned with my coffee and his ice water. She told Robert she was going to check on the kid and she disappeared down the hallway.

"Who killed Jack Minor?" I asked.

Reggie muttered, " 'Bout two in the mornin', me and Jack was on Church, walkin' toward Gay Street. They come walkin' up the other way. Three of 'em. One of 'em's singin'."

"Singing?"

"The big one. One big, one medium-sized, one little — scrawny kid."

"A kid?"

"They all kids. No more'n nineteen or twenty, I'd say. Drunk. They come up on me and Jack, and the big one say, 'Give me your hat, old man.'"

I swallowed. "He wanted the hat?"

Reggie nodded. "Jack told me somebody gave it to him, didn't even have to ask, just gave it. So Jack tells the kid, 'No; it's my hat.' Big kid, he starts shovin' Jack around, tryin' to grab it off his head. I say, 'Caddy, ain't worth it; give it up.' But Caddy don't listen. So 'nother one, the medium-sized one, he sneaks around Jack's backside while he slappin' with the big kid and grabs it off his head. So Jack goes after him, and the big one jumps him from behind." He set his glass on the floor between his feet and hid his face behind those large knuckles. "They took turns on him, 'cept the skinny one. He was like me, both of us yellin' for 'em to stop. Didn't do no good. Big one drug him into the parking lot, and the other one finds this two-by-four lyin' in the alley there . . . they take turns on him with that two-by-four, and the big one, he's wearing the hat. He's wearin' Jack's goddamned hat while he beats him to death!"

Reggie broke down then, putting his head between his knees, his narrow shoulders shaking. I looked over at Robert, who was looking back at me.

"What were you doing during all this?" I asked.

Reggie lifted his head and the look in his eyes forced me to look away.

"Nothin', Mr. Ruzak," he said. "Nothin' at all."

TWENTY-SIX

*T*he skinny kid noticed Reggie take off down Church, and shouted something to his buddies. One of them chased him down—Reggie wasn't sure which one—screaming, "You're next! You're next, motherfucker!" But the kid was drunk and gave up the chase after a few blocks. Reggie hid in the Hilton parking lot, debating whether to find a cop or return to the alley to check on his friend. After a couple of hours, he risked it, finding Jack and my hat in the alley behind the Ely. He left Jack there, but took the hat.

"Why didn't you go to the cops?" I asked.

"Ain't you been listenin'? They said they was goin' to kill me! I hitched a ride out of town at first light."

"That's not the only reason," Liz said gently.

"You were afraid they'd suspect you?" I asked Reggie.

"I been to prison six times," Reggie said. "Last time Bushy State. I ain't goin' back to prison."

"Can you describe them?"

"Big one, the hitter, he was blond, bright blond, like it was dyed, you know? Had a crew cut and a goatee. Medium one real small eyes, pig eyes, and the little guy, long hair down to his shoulders, baby-faced, hardly no chin. Don't remember much else. Big one wearing a UT sweatshirt but, you know," he shrugged. "It's football season."

"How about names? You catch any names?"

Reggie shook his head. "Called each other 'bro.'"

"'Bro' like *brother*?"

"Yeah, like *brother*."

I walked him through the story again, to see if he'd remember more detail and also to see if he remained consistent. He lost it again at the part where "the big one" found the two-by-four.

"Who is Yahweh?" I asked suddenly.

"Don't know any Yahweh."

"So you don't know what the letters Y-H-W-H mean?" I pressed.

He slowly shook his head. Robert said, "Okay, I'll bite. What do they mean?"

"Somebody took a sharp object and carved those letters into Jack's forehead," I said, looking at Reggie.

"Then they must've done it after I took off," Reggie said.

"Any idea why somebody would do that, Reggie?"

Again, he shook his head. He muttered something like "God, I need a drink," and lowered his head, hands kneading his bony knees.

Liz left the room. I sipped my cold coffee. Robert stared at me, and Reggie stared at his own lap.

"You have to go to the cops," I told him.

"No, Mr. Ruzak. No cops."

"You have to tell them what you saw."

"They'll kill me."

"I won't let that happen."

"They'll arrest me. They'll think I did it."

"They will question you," I said. "And maybe get your DNA and probably polygraph you. I can help you find a lawyer, if you want."

"I ain't nothing but a broken-down drunk, Mr. Ruzak, and the doctors got me on pills to control my moods now, but I ain't crazy."

"I know the detective in charge of the case. She's very sharp, and I also think she's very fair. I promise you she'll take you seriously."

"You can't promise that."

"What about Jack?" I asked. "Don't you want to do right by him?"

"Right by him?"

"You want them to get away with it, Reggie? Is that what you want? Because I guarantee you they will if you don't come forward. He's not high on their list, Reggie; the police aren't going to pursue this unless we make them, you and me. And you and me, we're all Jack has now. Are you going to turn your back on him?"

"There ain't nothin' I can do for him now."

I ignored him. Things that had been simmering were beginning to boil over the lip of the pot. "Maybe not, but if three kids on a lark can get away with beating a homeless man to death, we've reached the bottom of it. As low as we can get, and if you turn away now you're not just turning away from Jack, you're turning away from the next guy these kids decide to kill simply because they can.

"I don't know if you're a religious man. I'm not or never thought I was, but I've lost a lot of sleep since I saw the name of God on your friend's forehead, and I think it says somewhere in the Bible that what you do to the least of these you do to him, and you could look at it that way, if you're a religious man, that God was murdered that night. If he's in us and we're in him, God is murdered every night. And what's been getting to me is the fact that we've used up the not-knowing-what-we-do excuse. By God, if we don't know by now what we're doing, we're in big trouble and not just in the theological sense.

"We can't be as good as God and, if he's really there, I don't think he expects us to. I just think he expects us to be human—not as in a species, but as in his . . . crop. You know, the dinosaurs had their time—their season—now it's our season. It's our turn until he decides to let something else have a chance to get it right."

Liz returned during my rant, standing at the juncture between the hall and the family room, staring at me, a beat-up brown knapsack in one hand.

"What the hell was that?" Robert asked. "What the hell *was* that?"

"Sorry," I said.

TWENTY-SEVEN

*T*ake care of my old man, Ruzak," Robert told me at the door.
"Or I'll slap a wrongful death suit on your ass and you'll be
out a helluva lot more than twenty-five grand."

"I gotta kiss him good-bye," Reggie announced and shuffled
down the hall before anyone could stop him.

Liz put her hand on my arm. "Thank you, Mr. Ruzak," she
said. She was holding my hat. I took it from her but hesitated before setting it on my head. It didn't feel right, wearing evidence
to a capital crime.

"His pills are in the bag," Liz said. "Make sure he takes them.
And you better get rid of any alcohol in your house."

"He isn't allergic to dogs, is he?" I asked. "I have a short-hair,
but there may be dander issues."

She shook her head. "I don't know."

Reggie rested his gnarled hand on my forearm to steady himself on the way down the stairs. I could feel his son's eyes on the back of my head as we descended. First I adopted a dog, now a homeless man. I was going to need a bigger apartment if I kept this up.

At the intersection of State of Franklin Road, as we waited for the light to change, Reggie said, "You know Steve Spurrier, the football coach? He went to high school here. You like football, Mr. Ruzak?"

"I used to play it," I said.

"Yeah? What position?"

"Left guard."

"I could see that."

"I like to watch it—it's great to fall asleep to on a Sunday afternoon."

"Don't watch TV like I used to," Reggie said.

"Golf is good, too, for a nap," I said. "And tennis."

I pulled off the interstate to hit the Wendy's late-night drive-thru. I asked Reggie if he wanted anything. He leaned forward, squinting at the menu, rubbing his thighs.

"Oh, boy," he breathed. "Ain't been to Wendy's in years. They still have the Frosties?"

I ordered a medium Frostie for him and an Italian Frescata sandwich for me. I would have preferred a burger, but his bringing up football had made me uncomfortably cognizant of my size.

Back on the interstate, heading south, I gripped the wheel with one hand and my Frescata sandwich with the other. Reggie dug out dripping mounds of the nondairy frozen treat with his plastic spoon and sucked through pursed lips.

"Tell me about Jack," I said.

"I told you twice already."

"No, I mean the living Jack. What was he like?"

"Real good guy. Always shared what he had, no matter what it was. If he had a couple bucks and you were busted, he gave you one."

"He ever talk about his past?"

Reggie shook his head and his tongue darted between his lips. "Said he was in Nam. Lost everything when his old lady kicked him out for drinkin'."

"But where was he from? How'd he end up on the streets? What happened to him?"

Again, he shook his head. "Like I said, he didn't talk much."

I couldn't remember Reggie saying Jack didn't talk much, but this wasn't an interrogation and my job wasn't to lean on Reggie Matthews. He had that delicate air of someone breaking the grip of dependency. It hung around him, like a pall. You sense it in recovering addicts and jilted lovers, or anyone who's had their crutch abruptly yanked away.

"Was he religious?"

"Why's that matter?"

"His little sign mentioned God."

"That wasn't his. I made that sign."

"You let him use it?"

He nodded. "We worked that corner in shifts."

"So was he? Religious?"

"I never seen him pray or go to any church, if that's what you're askin'. He was retarded, you know. Not bad, but there was a lot he didn't get."

"I'm just having trouble understanding why one of those kids carved those letters into his face."

"Sick joke, you ask me."

He dropped his plastic fork into the empty cup and jammed it into the holder between the bucket seats.

"Now I'm cold," he complained, scrunching down and folding his arms over his chest. I cranked up the heat.

"Pretty esoteric joke," I said. "I don't know many people besides priests or rabbis or religion professors who'd get it."

The hairs on the back of my neck stood up. What a dufus you are, Ruzak, I told myself. I looked over at Reggie, hunkered down in the bucket seat, knees pressed together, squinting through the windshield as if we were on the road on a bright spring day.

In the art of detection, it's not just asking the right questions. You have to ask the right people the right questions.

"How far is the campus from the Ely Building?" I asked.

"How the hell would I know?"

"No more than a mile," I guessed. "Walking distance."

"All right," he drawled. He was waiting for the punch line. I didn't have it, but I suspected I knew who might.

TWENTY-EIGHT

I fetched a couple of old blankets I inherited from my dead mother to fix up the sofa for Reggie. He gave the middle cushion a tentative push. Then he announced he was still a little hungry, so I found a couple of Roma tomatoes in the crisper drawer, dropped a couple of pieces of bacon in the pan to fry, popped a couple slices of bread into the toaster, and tore the wilted edges from a couple of leaves of lettuce for a BLT. Reggie sat on the edge of the sofa and worried his hands in his lap.

"Where's your dog?" he asked.

"He's being sat by my secretary."

"Sat?"

"Well, it's a pretty long drive and he's a new dog. I didn't know how he'd handle it."

"Is he vicious?"

"Oh, no, but I wouldn't say he's issue-free. I adopted him—or somebody adopted him for me. That's more accurate."

I hadn't had a sleepover in years. Amanda had sort of offered. I wondered what it meant, if it meant anything, that I ran a girl out my door but welcomed with open arms a homeless man who might be a sadistic killer. Human beings have a tendency to read meaning into everything, like that woman a few years back in the Bible Belt who saw an image of the Virgin in the dried grease of her frying pan. Back in the fall, I read this story about a kid who threw his mom's cell phone in the microwave—I don't remember the reason, but the kid was a teenager—and Mary appeared in the ruined LCD. It would be odd for the Mother of God to choose to reveal herself in a cell phone, but once the story got around, pilgrims began to appear at their trailer.

Reggie ate his BLT at the kitchen counter, taking it with a tall glass of milk. I dug into his backpack and found the pill bottle.

"Here," I said, dropping a tablet by his elbow. "Says you're supposed to take it with food."

He grunted and tapped the pill with the nail of his index finger.

"Jumper's antijumping pill," he muttered.

"Why did you want to jump all those times?" I asked.

"Wouldn't you?"

I decided to change the subject. "Why did they call Jack Cadillac?"

He shrugged. "Maybe 'cause it rhymed."

"You really don't know that much about Jack, do you?"

"I know he had a taste for beef jerky. He liked baseball. He had arthritis and a bad leg. Said it was from shrapnel—friendly fire in Nam."

"The police checked into that," I said. "They didn't find any record of him in the service."

"Said he was a Marine."

"Maybe he just thought he was. Although I'm not sure retardation leads to delusions. Maybe he just lied."

Reggie sighed. "Does it matter?"

"I guess not."

"I still ain't really sure why I'm here."

"In the morning we're going down to KPD headquarters."

He shook his head. "No, I am not."

"I'll protect you," I said. "I have a gun."

"You gonna shoot our way out of the police station?"

"I meant I can protect you from Jack's killers."

He laughed a bitter bark of a laugh. "Where the hell did you come from, Ruzak?"

"Well, I was born in New York, but Dad moved us around a lot, always in the southerly direction. I guess if he'd lived longer I'd be in Key West."

I wondered if I was reading this old guy wrong. Maybe he killed Jack after an argument and that's why he was reluctant to talk to the police. He knew their skills in interrogation exceeded mine. Maybe the whole story of the marauding college kids was a lie. But why, then, come back to Knoxville with me? To dispatch the meddlesome gumshoe? Would someone—Felicia maybe—find me in a couple days, black and bloated in my bedsheets, God's name carved on my forehead?

I had forgotten to check messages, so while Reggie washed up for bed I listened to about thirty seconds of silence while whoever called hung on the line. The caller ID had registered the same thing as before: UNKNOWN CALLER. Someone was reaching out.

DECEMBER 6

TWENTY-NINE

I was on the phone with Felicia first thing in the morning. Actually, it was the second thing, after a cup of black coffee and a slice of toast with apple butter. For some reason, every time I had it, I thought of the first day of school.

"Why are you talking so softly? I can barely hear you," she said.

"I don't want to wake up Reggie."

"Who?"

"Jumper. I brought him home last night."

"And the reason you brought him home? . . ."

I told her. I also told her I was relieved I didn't wake up bludgeoned to death.

"Ruzak, if you were bludgeoned . . . never mind. When are you picking up this dog?"

"I'm swinging by right after I take care of Reggie."

"Good. I'm letting you deal with Tommy."

"Why am I dealing with Tommy?"

"You know why. You do it just to buy time, Ruzak, but what good is that?"

"Maybe it's the one thing you can buy but can't keep."

"Do you make this stuff up, or are you just regurgitating something you read in *Reader's Digest*?"

"That happens," I admitted. "I'll think of something and I'll get all excited and my ego tells me it's original. It's like a default setting if I can't remember if I read it somewhere. My dad subscribed to *Reader's Digest* for his bathroom reading, and those are chock-full of the pithy quotes. Dad always used to tell me not to eat anything bigger than my own head, and I always wondered if that came from *Reader's Digest*."

"I wish I could have met your father," Felicia said. "One thing I would ask him is, 'Why, Mr. Ruzak. *Why?*'"

"What if I brought him a stuffed dog?"

She stayed right with me. It was one of the things that I liked about her.

"I think he would throw that stuffed dog back in your face."

"This could be a sign," I said. "Maybe Archie wasn't meant for me."

"I'm not keeping this dog, Ruzak."

"I was just putting a feeler out."

Next, I called Detective Black.

"You found Jumper," she said.

"Reggie, right," I said. "He wants to talk."

"Does this mean I get the twenty-five grand?"

"He didn't do it. I'd tell you the whole story, but I don't want to compromise the case."

"How would that compromise the case, Mr. Ruzak?" I could detect a smile in the question, and I thought of those large canines.

"I don't want to create any unnecessary inconsistencies."

"Your statement implies there are *necessary* inconsistencies."

"See what I mean? How's ten for you?"

I woke up Reggie and told him he needed a shower before we left. He protested.

"I washed up last night," he said.

"And a shave," I said. "My stuff's in the cabinet beneath the sink."

"What is this?" he asked petulantly. "We goin' to a funeral?"

I fried him a couple eggs while he got ready. He was sitting at my counter, sopping up the runny yolk with a slice of toast, when my phone rang.

"Theodore," Eunice Shriver said. "I am coming over."

"Eunice," I said. "You can't come over."

"I am tired of chasing after you like Alice's rabbit."

"I won't be here," I said.

"You will be there if I say you'll be there!"

She slammed the phone down. Reggie was staring at me, a dab

of egg quivering on his freshly shaved chin. He looked younger without the stubble; most older guys do.

"Who was that?" he asked.

"A god from an alternative string," I said as I flipped to the *S*'s in the phone book. I looked at my watch; I didn't have time to get into anything protracted, but an intervention seemed to be imperative.

"A what from a what?"

"Or maybe she would be a goddess, but the thing about the pantheists is their deities never made anything from scratch; it was always earthier than that, like Zeus frolicking with all those mortal women."

He picked up on the sixth ring. He didn't sound happy to be picking up.

"What?" he barked.

"Is this Vernon Shriver?" I asked.

"Who wants to know?" He possessed the native accent, slightly nasal, sharp in the middle, rough on the edges, like a hunk of half-grated cheese.

"Teddy Ruzak. I'm a . . ." What was I? ". . . a friend of your mom's."

"Did you say Ruzak?"

"Teddy Ruzak, that's right."

"Listen, buddy, I don't know who you are, but this isn't funny."

"It isn't?"

"You're from her workshop at the university, aren't you? Some wise-ass college kid."

"I'm a bit long in the tooth for that. The reason I was calling—"

"Mister, I don't have time for your jokes. Teddy Ruzak is the name of a character from Mom's book, so tell me what you want and stop yanking my chain. I'm late for work."

"I'm in the book," I offered.

"I know you're in the friggin' book; I just said that!"

"I meant the phone book," I said. "You can look me up."

"So Mom pulled the name out of the phone book. What's that prove?"

"Well, I guess that's my dilemma at the moment," I answered. "Trying to prove I exist. *Cogito, ergo sum.*"

"Huh?"

"Let's hang up, you call the number for Teddy Ruzak, I'll answer, and there you'll have it."

"I'm not calling anyone. I'm late."

"Then I'll be quick. Your mother just got off the phone with me and I'm a little worried about her."

"Ain't we all, pal."

"No, I mean seriously worried. I know I just said 'a little,' but really I mean seriously. I think there's been a break from reality."

"Ruzak—or whatever your name is—my mother's grip on reality's been loose for the past twenty-five years."

The line went dead. "You know," I said to Reggie. "Ultimately, there's only so much one person can do."

"And it ain't never nearly enough," he said, and I thought maybe I had found a kindred spirit, a fellow amateur philosopher, here in this very oddest of circumstances. But then, I thought, that's where you usually find the most kindred of spirits.

"But you have to try," I said. "Otherwise, you might as well be a fictional character. Though they tend to try harder than us."

"I couldn't save him," he said, his lower lip coming forward slightly, quivering in agitation. "I had to run. They would've killed me if I didn't."

"Look, Reggie, the police want these monsters off the street as badly as you do."

"This ain't gonna get them off the street," he said. "It was dark, I was drunk, and I got no names. What's the police gonna do? Round up every kid at UT? All this is gonna do is let 'em know I talked and then I don't care how many locks you got on this door or how many guns you got stashed under your pillow."

"Maybe you could ask them for some protection."

"Right, like they're gonna protect somebody like me."

"Maybe you should knock over a liquor store. That way they'd have to arrest you, kind of a de facto custody arrangement."

He got a funny look when I said that. I interpreted it as fear.

"Everything's going to be okay," I said.

"That's not a bad idea," he replied.

THIRTY

A uniformed female officer led Reggie and me through the doors marked AUTHORIZED PERSONNEL ONLY, down a long corridor, then into a conference room with armless, thin-cushioned folding chairs around a church social–type folding table. She took our drink orders, and after a couple of minutes returned with stale, weak coffee in white Styrofoam cups. She promised it would be just a couple more minutes and closed the door behind her.

"Relax," I told Reggie, whose bottom lip was edging out again.

The door opened and Detective Black came in with two men in tow, one in his shirtsleeves, a badge hanging just below his prodigious gut. The other was wearing a suit. Tailored. With gleaming Florsheims below his cuffs.

She made the introductions with an arctic smile that re-minded me it had been over two years since I'd been to the den-tist. What was wrong with me? Humans don't usually crash spectacularly, which was why, when they do, it's such startling news. We tend to crumple more than fall, a slow descent into chaos that actually accelerates after our end. The absolute still-ness of Jack Minor lying in that alley was deceptive. A human ca-daver is a busy thing as the organs and tissues break down.

The suit's name was Beecham, and he was with the district at-torney's office. The guy with the belly was Detective Louis Kennard.

As Detective Black checked the batteries on her tape recorder, Kennard turned to Reggie and said, "Hey, Jumper. Remember me?"

Reggie shook his head, lower lip now in full protuberance mode. His eyes were on the tabletop.

"I pulled you off the roof of the Marriot in '98."

Reggie didn't move a muscle. I said, "He's a little shaken up by all this. But he's going to cooperate. Right, Reggie?"

"I'm sorry," Beecham said. "Are you his attorney, Mr. Ruzak?"

"Not exactly."

"Not exactly," he echoed. "Then what exactly are you?"

"Well, I was an investigative consultant. For about nine months. Then the state closed me down over a technicality and now, you know, I like to keep my hand in."

"Mr. Ruzak is offering a reward for Jack's killer," Detective Black said. "I suppose he's here to protect his investment."

Beecham leaned over and whispered something to Meredith Black. She whispered something back. Kennard was smiling smugly, massive forearms folded across his chest. His cologne was very strong.

Finally, Beecham broke off the discussion with Meredith and said to me, "We'd like to talk to Mr. Matthews alone."

"Oh, no way," Reggie said. "Ruzak stays or I go."

"Try and I'll arrest you," Kennard said pleasantly.

"Here is the situation, Mr. Ruzak," Beecham said reasonably. "Mr. Matthews is here to give a statement. He's not under arrest, but it's totally outside the department's protocol to question a witness in the presence of a third party."

Reggie gave me a desperate look, as if to say, *Don't go!* I reached across the table and patted his hand before standing up.

"I'll be right outside," I said, more to him than to them. Detective Black opened the door for me and then closed it behind me. I lowered myself into the chair in the hallway beside the door, the little foam cup in my big hand, and steeled myself for the wait. I had read somewhere that the average person spends three years waiting—in lines, at traffic lights, on the phone, in the doctor's office—a fact that was both distressing and useless. I had been running into a lot of those kinds of facts lately. I wondered if Eunice was camping out on my doorstep, red pencil hovering over my ejaculations, poised for the coup d'état—or would that be more of a coup de grâce?

Thinking of Eunice brought on this panicky feeling in my gut, as if my own thoughts didn't belong to me, and I tried to comfort myself with that old saw about fearing for your sanity confirms that you're just fine, that crazy people never think they're crazy. Going crazy wasn't like coming down with a cold—but that was hardly comforting. I told myself I should be more myopic when it came to my understanding of reality. Most people are—painfully so. I suspected I was trying to keep too many balls in the meta-physical air. I couldn't seem to discard even the most worthless bit of information, like the fact that Einstein's brain weighed less than the average human's. Or that the higher your IQ, the more zinc and copper are contained in your hair. Or that every day we fart out a pint of gas. There's only so many neurons in the human brain (about a hundred billion), and I was loading them up with crap. What did it matter that blondes had more hair than brunettes or redheads? How was that going to help?

I had been sitting in that hallway for nearly an hour when the door opened and Meredith Black stepped out. I stood up.

"It's okay," she said. "He's agreed to take a polygraph."

"Why are you giving him a polygraph?"

"It's SOP."

"What about a sketch artist?"

"What *about* a sketch artist?"

"To get some composites of the guys who did this."

She gave my forearm a reassuring pat. "One thing at a time, Mr. Ruzak. Look, this is going to take a while. Why don't you let us give you a call when we're done?"

I looked at my watch. "There is one thing I need to do," I said. Something felt squirrelly about this, something about the set of this detective's jaw, but I couldn't put my finger on it. Besides, if things got really hinky I was sure Reggie would demand to see a lawyer.

"Call me on my cell," I told her.

"Of course," she said. She flicked a smile at me as casually as a lifelong smoker flicks his Bic.

"Okay," I said, not moving. "Okay, okay. I'll be back in a couple of hours."

"It would be better," she said, "if you waited for my call."

THIRTY-ONE

T he tetragrammaton," I said to Dr. Heifitz, "is hardly common knowledge. You remember saying that?"

The harsh late-morning light of early December shone through the smudged window behind me, and the shadows of the bobble-headed icons were long on the credenza.

He gave a quick, impatient nod of his weathered pate.

"And what is your point, Mr. Ruzak?" he asked, shaking his dice; I could hear them clicking together inside his fist.

"I have a witness who says the killers were college-aged kids."

"Killers? There was more than one?"

"Three young males."

"And you suspect something along the lines of a Yahweh death cult?"

"Well, I wouldn't rule out that possibility, though my witness says they behaved more like drunken rowdies than religious fanatics."

"As I think I told you, Mr. Ruzak, I know of no sect or cult that specifically emphasizes ritual sacrifice in the name of Yahweh."

"Right, and that's not why I'm here. I'm here because there's also a possibility that at least one of these young men, given the location of the crime and the ages of the perpetrators, was a college student."

"Ah." He leaned back in his chair, lacing his pale, thin fingers together in front of his chin. "Ah."

"And not just your run-of-the-mill undergrad frat boy. Someone either with a background steeped in some pretty obscure religious esoterica or maybe—and that's why I'm here—maybe someone who's taken a few religion classes. . . ."

"You're asking me if I think one of my students could be involved."

"You ever cover the tetragrammaton in class?"

He nodded slowly. "I have. It's part of a graduate lecture series on Judaism offered every spring."

He closed his eyes while I described the three guys Reggie saw, as if to better picture them in his mind. Then his eyes opened and he slowly shook his head.

"I'm sorry, Mr. Ruzak. After thirty-five years of teaching, the faces begin to blend into a single amalgamation: Adam the undergrad, if you will."

"So you don't recollect any odd kind of kid maybe a little fixated on God?"

"Being fixated on God is not odd, Mr. Ruzak. Or if it is, most of us are odd, then. Ninety-six percent of Americans profess a faith in the deity."

"I'll have to take your word on that," I said. "Though that's one of those statistics that gives you hope and bums you out at the same time. If everybody is buying into the system, why is the system so troubled?"

"I," he said, "am not troubled."

"What do you think . . . how difficult would it be for me to get my hands on the class roster for last spring?"

"All our rosters contain personal information zealously guarded by the university, Mr. Ruzak."

"You could black out the personal stuff," I said. "I just need the names. Phone numbers would help, too."

"I'll have to get it from the registrar's office. It might take a day or two."

He showed me to the door. I turned at the threshold to confide, "I think I'm in that tiny percentage who can't decide the question one way or the other."

"I like to comfort myself in such times with the fact that it hardly matters."

"How so?"

"If God exists, our belief or disbelief has no consequence."

"I always heard it did, in terms of where we spend eternity. But that gives me some hope, Professor. You know, there's this old lady who thinks I don't exist, at least on the physical plane, that I'm a figment of her imagination."

He showed me his large yellow teeth. "Perhaps I should pinch you."

"I suffer, therefore I am? But it could be the pain is part of her creation, too."

"It certainly is part of God's," he replied.

"I thought all that was Adam's fault."

"Yet the creation is still God's. If it isn't, we're in one helluva pickle, aren't we, Mr. Ruzak?"

THIRTY-TWO

*W*hat do you think?" I asked Felicia. "When you're eighty, will you be more or less anxious about eternity?"

"I think I'll be damned tired. Where are you, Ruzak?"

"Stuck in traffic on the Pike." Over two hours had passed since I left the police station and Detective Black still hadn't called. Thinking maybe she had tried my home number, I retrieved my messages, but all I had was two hang-ups, which I was sure came from Unknown Caller, and a long sales pitch from a company in New Jersey, offering me a once-in-a-lifetime deal in stock futures. If I ever had real money, the first thing I'd do is dump it in the lap of a fancy-pants investment counselor with a single order to sink it so far out of my reach it would take a bull-dozer to dig it out.

"Any idea when you might be by to get this animal? I don't need a specific time, just an ETA before midnight."

"Right after I pick up Reggie. They were setting up a polygraph when I left. It's making me a little nervous."

"How come?"

"They didn't polygraph me."

She laughed for some reason. I told her about my meeting with Dr. Heifitz. Then I told her about the hang-ups at home and Unknown Caller.

"You're about to share a hypothetical," she said.

"Here it is: three college kids on a drunk stumble across Jack and Reggie on Church Avenue. At least one of them attended the professor's seminar on ancient Jewish apocrypha, and in a burst of regret or maybe just to toss in a red herring, cuts the tetragrammaton into the old guy's forehead. But one of them, maybe the same one who cut God's name, is having trouble dealing with what they've done, and one day sees my poster on campus. He calls my number, but then he can't make himself say anything."

"Hmmm," she said, though "*hmmm*" isn't technically a word. "Here's an alternative hypo: Reggie got in a fight with Jack over your hat, killed him, and made up the whole story about the kids to cover his murderous ass."

"I would hate to think my hat was the spark."

"It's in your hypo, too."

"That part wasn't hypothetical. Reggie said those guys wanted my hat."

"It all boils down to your misplaced philanthropy."

"But if you went through life avoiding unintended conse-
quences, you'd never get a damn thing accomplished." I lifted my
foot off the brake pedal and inched forward about half a car
length. Why did I come this way? If I had her number, I'd call
Eunice Shriver and tell her to write me onto I-40. I wondered
how people would behave if our theology contained a promise
from God that he would answer just one prayer in their lifetime.

"Do you ever pray?" I asked Felicia.

"Every Saturday, right before they draw the lottery numbers."

"I guess I do, just not formally. Sometimes, stuck in traffic like
now, I go, 'Please, oh please,' and I guess that's a kind of prayer."

"Weird. I was having one of those this very moment. Please.
Oh, please."

"Okay," I said. I promised I'd call as soon as I got Reggie back
from the clutches of the curiously thorough Knoxville PD.

Forty-five minutes later, I was standing at the front desk sign-
ing in, when the double doors leading to the back swung open
and the big-bellied Detective Kennard stuck his conical-shaped
head through the opening.

"Ruzak!" he barked. He crooked his finger at me, but he didn't
step aside to let me pass.

"You may want to hang out here for a while," he said. I smelled
garlic on his breath. "He's downstairs getting booked."

Stupidly, I said, "Who's getting booked?"

"Jumper. He says he wants to talk to you, but we gotta get him processed first."

"Why did you arrest him?"

"He confessed."

"That's impossible."

"Think so?"

"I want to talk to him."

"You're not listening, Ruzak. I just said after we process him."

"I want to talk to Detective Black."

"She's at lunch."

"It's two-thirty in the afternoon."

"Late lunch."

He waited for me to say something else. I didn't have something else to say. He left and I sat in the small waiting area and flipped through an old *People* magazine while I waited. Ten pages were devoted to Oscar Night's fashion flubs.

What now? Dear God, what now? Had I read it all wrong? He did run when Jack died, but why would he come back if he was guilty? Did he figure if some thickheaded out-of-work PI could track him down, the Knoxville PD certainly could? Maybe they showed him the crime scene photos and he collapsed in a paroxysm of remorse. His relationship with his son wasn't peachy, to say the least. He must have known if he showed up on his stoop fessing up to murder, Robert would probably turn him in, so he invented the drunk-frat-boys story as cover.

A uniformed officer escorted me to the visitors' room. Reggie was waiting on the other side of the glass, dressed in an orange jumpsuit, the receiver already pressed to his ear.

I picked up the receiver on my side and said, "What happened?"

"They arrested me, Ruzak, what do you think happened?"

"Did you kill him, Reggie?"

He stared at me for ten agonized seconds, and then began to cry and laugh, both at once, and I noticed for the first time that Reggie Matthews was missing most of his teeth.

"Just don't tell Bobby," he cried. "Don't tell my boy. It'll break his heart, Ruzak. It'll break his heart."

And that's all I got from Reggie Matthews, besides the mixture of laughter and tears, and I thought of those mammoth, gravity-defying roller coasters, the ones where your feet dangle in empty space as your body is whipped and spun around, and you worry about your wallet falling out of your back pocket, and the way we scream through that controlled fall, the one we normally endure, when you think about it, with someone we love by our side.

THIRTY-THREE

Detective Black closed the door to her office and, as she passed me on the way to her chair, I caught a whiff of her perfume, causing a swelling in my nasal cavities.

"What happened?" I asked.

"He confessed."

"And you believe him?"

"Of course not, but I decided to arrest him anyway."

"Detective Black—"

"Please, call me Meredith."

"Okay, Meredith . . . nobody could ever accuse me of being the most logical person who ever came down the pike, but the 'why's' don't make any sense to me."

"What do you mean?"

"Either his confession is true or it isn't. If it is true, why did he come down here today? If it isn't true, why would he lie?"

She stared at me for a second before answering. "The only thing I know, Mr. Ruzak, is Reggie Matthews admitted to taking a piece of two-by-four to Jack Minor's head."

"He didn't have to come," I said. "I didn't tie him up and drive him over here in my trunk. Why would he make a big show of cooperating and then confess to murder? But if he is innocent, what happened in that room after I left which would make him confess to a capital crime?"

"Boy," she said. "You got me. We did show him the crime scene photos. After that, he broke down and told us the truth."

"The truth."

"The truth," she repeated, nodding.

"He beat his best friend to death."

"That's right."

"Over my hat," I said.

"He didn't say what started the argument."

"Then Reggie took a broken piece of glass and carved God's initials into Jack's forehead."

She shrugged. "We didn't discuss that."

"Why?"

"Does it matter?"

"I think it does."

"Well, you're not the lead detective on the case, are you?"

"Something's wrong here," I said.

"No, something has finally gone right here. Solving a crime is what we detectives call a good thing."

"Unless the solution is based on a coerced confession."

"I take great offense at that, Mr. Ruzak."

"Well, I take great offense at this whole setup. I could see two buddies having a falling out. I could even see Reggie beating him—though it goes against my gut; Reggie doesn't strike me as the violent type—but I can't see him mutilating the body like that. For one thing, I don't think Reggie Matthews knows Yahweh from a hole in the ground."

She didn't say anything. The teeth were out, though.

I went on. "I haven't been a detective very long, not even a year. Well, I was never really a detective beyond the most generic definition of the word, but don't the elements of a crime have to fit into its solution?"

"Mr. Ruzak, there are some elements to every crime that remain mysteries."

"You people pushed him. You wore him down. That's why you got me out of that room."

"Who are you?" she asked. "Are you Mr. Matthew's attorney? Are you related to the suspect in any way? You're not a detective, you just told me that, so who are you, and what is your business in this case?"

"I just want Jack's killer," I said. "That's all I want."

"Me, too. And I think I got him. You may think otherwise, and on that we'll just have to agree to disagree, Mr. Ruzak, and let a court of law decide who's right. In the meantime, maybe you can use that twenty-five thousand dollars you saved today to hire an attorney for Mr. Matthews. Since you're so convinced of his innocence."

"I'm not convinced of anything," I said, rising from my chair. "Except this: If Reggie Matthews is innocent and you guys are innocent, there's only one reason he'd confess to a crime he didn't commit."

I made for the door, walking on the balls of my feet, like a sprinter cooling down from a dash, strangely lightheaded, with a tingling in my fingertips.

"What's the reason?" she called after me.

"Fear," I said.

THIRTY-FOUR

I called Felicia from the car. I got her voice mail. I left a message.

"Hey. It's me. Ruzak. Teddy. You know . . . hey, Reggie confessed. I'm not sure what that's about, but I'm pretty sure he pulled this for a little protective custody. Maybe he's thinking he can recant at any point and they'll have to let him go. Or maybe he is guilty and I'm just plucking at straws because *I* can't let this go. Anyway, I thought if you were around I could pick up the dog. Thanks. Okay. I'll be at my place. 'Bye."

The cold front had followed me down from Johnson City; the temperature hovered around twenty and the radio warned of a hard freeze coming. Everything, from the traffic lights to the naked branches of the dogwoods, had that terrible stillness, that sharply etched quality of a photograph that made you feel like a voyeuristic interloper in a landscape at once familiar and alien, like a lonely man looking at a picture of a beautiful woman.

A small figure in a worn gray coat was huddled on the stoop of the Sterchi Building as I pulled into the lot. I wondered why she didn't wait in her car; she could at least keep warm that way.

"Eunice," I said, my six-foot-five frame towering over her small, gray, bent-backed lump. "Eunice, what are you doing?"

I noticed her white wig was slightly askew. She raised her head so I could see her face, the nose a startlingly bright red, the rheumy eyes squinting, although most of the light had already bled from the day.

"*You*," she muttered, as if I was the last person she expected to see on the front stoop of his own apartment building.

"Come on," I said. "I'll brew you a nice hot cup of tea."

I slid my hand beneath her elbow and pulled her up. She was heavier than I expected; maybe it was all the layers of clothing, the gray coat, the matching gray muffler, the man's red flannel shirt, the athletic sweats with the elastic bands at the ankles. She grabbed the ubiquitous tote and slung it over her shoulder as we eased our way across the frozen concrete to the front doors.

Upstairs, she collapsed on the sofa, cradling the canvas tote in her lap, the tan blotches on her hands sharply contrasted against the paleness of her skin. I set a pot of water on the stove to boil and positioned only half my butt on the bar stool at the counter: You never know when you might have to make a break for it.

"I talked to Vernon this morning," I told her.

"I don't know anything about that conversation," she said.

"He doesn't believe I'm real."

She waved her left hand in a gesture of dismissal. The right maintained its death grip on the tote.

"Why should he, after all?" She wasn't looking at me. She had that "third space" stare of a prophet—or a mystic, I guess, since we don't live in an age of prophets.

"I guess there's nothing that says he has to," I said. "Though it would be nice."

"I am very angry with you, Theodore," she said.

"Well," I said.

"And disappointed. You have deeply disappointed me."

"Eunice, I never asked you to write a book about me."

"About you," she snapped. "About *you*. Oh, I am sick to death of you, Theodore Ruzak!"

She hurled the tote at my head. I ducked. It skittered across the bar and landed on the kitchen floor, disgorging a stack of paper that spread out, fanlike, across the linoleum.

I picked up the top sheet and read the first sentence: "I'd had this dopey idea to be a detective ever since my mother gave me an illustrated Sherlock Holmes book for my tenth birthday." It wasn't the sort of sentence that compelled me to read on, but I'm no literary critic.

Behind me, Eunice Shriver continued to rant.

"It's ridiculous. Absolutely ridiculous! No detective in history has been so woefully underqualified, distracted, lazy, and incompetent. What person in their right mind is going to believe you set up shop as a private eye without even realizing you needed a license?"

"Fools rush in?"

"I can always change your looks. Make you thinner, chiseled, steely-eyed. I toyed with making your eyes steel-gray, as a matter of fact. But I cannot change these basic character flaws that *in themselves* make you completely unbelievable as a character!"

"Look at it this way," I offered, shoving the stack of paper back into the tote. "You're plowing new ground."

"Here is the thing," she barked, still not looking in my direction. "Your story . . . if you want to call it that, has less substance than a takeout menu."

"Then let it go."

She swung her gaze in my direction, but still wouldn't look directly at my face. Her eyes were focused on some point just over my head.

"Eunice," I said. I went to the sofa and lowered myself into the cushions beside her. I pulled her cold, withered hand into mine. "Eunice. I'm going to pose a simple hypothetical."

"Fat chance!"

"What if you just went to bed and when you got up it was gone? Would you be sad or relieved?"

"Both. I cannot abandon you in midstream, Theodore. It would be like God stopping with the fishes."

"I'm sensing a disconnect here. Between you and God and me and the . . . the fishes. Do you feel my hand, Eunice?"

She didn't say anything.

I rubbed her hand hard between both of mine, feeling her arthritic knuckles slide beneath my palms.

"I'm real, Eunice. I have an existence outside your imagination."

"That is a terrifying thought," she said.

I was about to ask her why when my buzzer sounded. It broke the existential spell. I swung through the kitchen on the way to the intercom to turn off the burner; the water was boiling over the lip of the pot.

"Ruzak?"

"Amanda?"

"Amanda?" Eunice called from the sofa. "I know of no Amanda!"

"Can I come up?" Amanda asked.

"Right now?"

"No, not now. I thought I'd just ask now and come back in a couple of hours."

"Come on up," I said, and hit the green button. I returned to the kitchen to drop the teabag in Eunice's cup.

When the knock came on the door, Eunice said, a bit panicky, "Who could that be?"

Amanda stood in the hallway holding a white plastic bag with THANK YOU! written in red on the outside.

"I'm hoping you haven't eaten," she said.

"I haven't," I said, and stepped to one side so she could pass. I caught a whiff of fried rice. Amanda stopped when she saw Eunice on my sofa.

"Oh," she said.

"Amanda, this is Eunice Shriver, no relation to the famous Shrivers."

"That Maria is an anorexic so help me God!" Eunice cried.

"Maybe this isn't a good time," Amanda said.

"I can't think of a more perfect one," I said, taking the bag from her and setting it on the coffee table, about a foot from Eunice's broad knees. "You like hot tea? I'm guessing this is Chinese."

Amanda nodded. She eased herself onto the edge of a bar stool, staring at Eunice. I refilled the pot and turned on the burner. I kept meaning to invest in a teakettle.

"I detest Chinese food," Eunice told Amanda.

"I didn't know," Amanda said.

"Gives me the runs."

"Maybe you got hold of some bad noodles," I said. "I have some Campbell's in the pantry."

"Chicken noodle?"

"I think it's cream of potato."

"Dear God!" She made a sour face. Amanda gave me a look.

"It's a very long story," I told her. "Eunice, how about a grilled cheese sandwich?"

So that's how we supped: Amanda and I on noodles and rice,

sitting crossed-legged at the coffee table, Eunice on grilled cheese and baby dills, the dish in her lap.

"Where's Archie?" Amanda asked.

"Sleepover," I said.

"Who is Archie?" Eunice demanded. "Who are all these people I don't know, Theodore?"

"Is this your grandmother or something?" Amanda asked.

"I am his creator!" Eunice said, not without a touch of pride.

"Eunice is writing a book about me," I said.

"She is? Why?"

"I'm still not sure. This is really good," I said, meaning the food. "You didn't have to."

"I took a chance you'd be here. I wanted to apologize for last time."

"What happened last time?" Eunice asked.

"You should know," I said. "That's what I've been trying to tell you, Eunice. If this was all in your head, how could there be things that you don't know?"

"I'll tell you, if you'll give me a complete inventory of the contents of your hall closet."

"I'm not following this," Amanda said.

"It's a philosophical dilemma," I said. "Right up your alley."

"It seems more psychological."

"But physiology is muscling that out," I said. "Everything's getting traced back to whacked-out brain chemistry."

"I don't want you to hate me, Ruzak," Amanda said.

"I don't."

"I want to be your friend."

"You are."

Eunice was watching us, pivoting her head, a tennis match.

"We could slow it down a little. I can move fast sometimes, I know that," Amanda said.

"Right."

"It's just you're not like other guys I've dated. I've been conditioned, you know? A burger, a movie, and right to the mattress."

I cleared my throat. I would have been uncomfortable with this without Eunice Shriver sitting two feet away.

"I just don't want to give you the wrong impression," I said. "It's like I said before: It goes against my general principles to get wrapped up while I'm untangling some issues."

"Sometimes it helps, though, having someone there to help you untangle them."

"I can't deny that."

"Teddy Ruzak does not have a love life!" Eunice interjected.

"That's what we're working on," Amanda said with a smile. Smiling wasn't something she did often but, when she did, it was a good smile.

"He is as celibate as a monk!"

"Tell me about it," Amanda said.

"Theodore Ruzak has not had sexual relations since 1998!"

"Whoa," Amanda said. "Really?"

I didn't say anything. Any answer would be humiliating.

"Did Miss Marple have a lover? Hercule Poirot? Did the greatest detective of all time, Sherlock Holmes, have a sweetie?" Eunice's chin rose indignantly.

"Well, I always wondered about him and Watson," Amanda said.

"Watson got married," I pointed out.

"And your point?" Amanda asked.

Eunice said, "Theodore, I have not formed a good impression of this girl."

"Oh, no," Amanda said.

"She should be discarded."

"But you don't even know me," Amanda said, reasonably.

"Oh, I know you," Eunice said. "I know you."

"I get it," Amanda whispered to me. "It has its own interior logic. Since you're her creation, anything connected to you is part of it, too."

I shrugged. It had come to that. Shrugging.

"Well," I said. "You're the philosophy major. I've been hugging Descartes like a long-lost brother lately. How do I know she isn't right? How do I ultimately confirm my own existence?"

Amanda stared at me for a second, a smile playing at the corner of her lips. Then she leaned toward me, grabbed my face in both her hands, and pressed her lips against mine. I tasted pork-fried rice. From the sofa, I heard Eunice gasp. Amanda pulled away, no more than a couple of inches, so her loamy eyes filled my vision.

"Now what, Ruzak?" she murmured.

It struck me how uninhibited she was, even at the feet of

crazy ol' Eunice Shriver, who, for all Amanda knew, was perfectly capable of grabbing a carving knife from my kitchen and plunging it into her recalcitrant back.

"That is better," I said.

At that moment, my cell phone rang. I fumbled for it. Amanda leaned back and sipped the dregs of her tea. Eunice watched me, open-mouthed.

"Ruzak, where are you?" Felicia asked.

"Home," I said.

"Why didn't you call me?"

"I did. I left you a voice mail."

"Well, I haven't been home; what did you expect?"

"I wasn't expecting much of anything, really."

"Look, Tommy and I and this damn dog are four blocks away."

"Four blocks away from what?"

"From you, dummy. I'm picking up Bob from work." Bob worked at the fire station downtown, about six blocks from the Sterchi.

"Who is that?" Eunice asked from the sofa.

"Who is that?" Felicia asked on the phone.

"Felicia," I said to Eunice.

"What?" Felicia asked.

"Felicia?" Eunice asked.

"Who's Felicia?" Amanda asked.

"Who's that?" Felicia asked.

"Eunice," I said to Felicia.

"Ruzak, that didn't sound like an eighty-six-year-old woman to me," Felicia said.

"Oh. Amanda," I said.

"What?" Amanda asked.

"I'm telling Felicia your name," I said.

"The dog philosopher?" Felicia asked. "And Eunice? How many strays are you going to take in, Ruzak?"

"Hmmm," I said. All eyes were upon me. "Nothing's been planned, really."

"Is that the girlfriend?" Amanda asked.

"There is no girlfriend, per se," I managed to get out.

"Damn right!" Eunice ejaculated.

"Ruzak, did you tell her I was your girlfriend?" Felicia asked.

"Of course not," I said. "Maybe you should swing by tomorrow."

"This isn't good for Tommy," she said, meaning the situation with Archie. "The sooner he's back with you, the better."

She hung up. I set the phone on the kitchen counter.

"Felicia, my secretary," I said. "She's bringing Archie back."

"Who is Archie?" Eunice asked.

"Ruzak's dog," Amanda said.

"Theodore doesn't own a dog," Eunice said. "It would be completely contradictory to his character."

That did it. I picked up the phone and dialed Vernon's number.

"Vernon," I said after he had barked that East Tennessean version of a greeting: *Hell-uh!* "This is Teddy Ruzak and I have your mother."

I heard him take a deep breath. "You are one sick—"

I cut him off. "Here, she wants to talk to you."

I held the phone toward her and she commenced to frantically waving her hands, like a football referee signaling the end of a play. She mouthed the word *no*.

"Well," I said into the phone. "I guess she doesn't. But you need to come over. You got something to write with? I'll give you my address."

"I'm callin' the FBI," he promised.

"I'm thinking the psychiatric ward at Saint Mary's might be more appropriate."

"You think this is funny, don't you?"

"I don't think it's funny at all, Vernon. It's downright disturbing . . . on so many levels."

I gave him my address.

"If this ain't on the up-and-up, I'm prosecuting you, mister," he promised before hanging up.

"I won't go," Eunice told me.

"You have to," I said. "He's your flesh and blood, Eunice. I'm neither, in either possible universe. He can get you some help."

My buzzer sounded. Felicia and the dog. I buzzed her up. Amanda pulled me aside and said, "Tell me the truth. She's the one you told me about, isn't she?"

"She's my secretary," I said. "She has a boyfriend."

"You have a thing for her. You can hear it in your voice."

"Really? No, I just like her, that's all. She has pleasant knees."

"Pleasant knees?"

"You know, well formed."

"Oh, Christ."

"You should understand the year 1998 was just a supposition."

The door burst open and Tommy barreled into the room shouting my name, "Roo-zack! Roo-zack!" and, behind him, Archie the beagle mix, trying hard to keep up, putting its front feet on Tommy's rear while the kid pawed at me. Felicia hovered in the doorway, taking in the scene.

"Hi," Amanda said to Felicia. "You must be Ruzak's crush."

Felicia gave me a look. Amanda smiled and said, "Your pleasant knees gave you away."

Eunice glared at Felicia. "Hello, and how are you, little Miss Felicia?"

"Well, Ruzak," Felicia said. "I guess one of those cosmic strings is unraveling, isn't it?"

THIRTY-FIVE

*I*t was an awkward situation, more of a tangling of the various strands than an unraveling. Amanda's was the first to peel away: she crooked her finger at me and I followed her into the hallway.

"Be honest with me, Ruzak," she said. "Is there anything here worth pursuing?"

"What do you think?"

"Don't answer my question with a question."

"Socratic method," I said, hoping to make a philosophical connection. That's life's rub, connection. Between the dog and Eunice and even Jack with the staring eyes beneath God's name was Teddy Ruzak clutching the tugging butt-ends of the balloon strings as they urged him upward toward . . . what? You wondered sometimes if life was just a slow rush toward gibberish.

"What? Ruzak, do you ever get at what you really mean?"

"It's been a lifelong struggle," I admitted.

I offered to escort her to her car; downtown Knoxville can be scary at night, but she acted offended at my offer. As she walked to the stairs, I watched, admittedly, her rear end.

Back in my apartment, I discovered Archie in Eunice's lap, Tommy squatting at her feet, and Felicia sitting on one of the bar stools, her expression bemused.

"Vernon's on his way to pick her up," I told Felicia, with a nod toward the old lady.

"You told that girl you had a crush on me?" she asked.

"She's extrapolating."

"From what?"

"From a lie."

"What lie?"

"I told her I had a girlfriend."

"Don't get a crush on me, Ruzak. Where's the street person you took in?"

"They arrested him."

"Why?" Felicia asked.

"He confessed."

"Good," Felicia said. "Case closed."

"I think he's lying," I said.

"Why would someone lie about that?"

"I'm working on the answer, but I think it has something to do with fear."

Vernon Shriver arrived thirty-five minutes later. He was pushing forty, with a wide, flat face and smallish eyes, short like his mother, but I didn't see much of a resemblance, so maybe his looks came from the Shriver side.

"You Ruzak?" he asked at the door, as if he still wasn't quite buying this whole setup. I told him I was, in the flesh, and the tripartite talks began in earnest. Vernon seemed more interested in getting her to accept my autonomy than getting her out the door, which was my ultimate goal. He kept slapping me on the forearm, saying things like, "I feel him, Momma; he's right here; how could I feel him if he wasn't here?" But it was like four-foot swells crashing against a seawall. Eunice refused to budge, from either her convictions or my sofa.

"What about going to Vernon's place?" I asked. "You could stay with him for a few days." I took him aside and said, "She can't stay here and can't be alone. What choice do you have?"

"This is messed up," he said. "You messed her up, Ruzak. I'm gonna look into this." I wasn't sure what he meant by that.

Felicia sat beside Eunice and spoke to her quietly while Vernon and I argued. Tommy enticed Archie from Eunice's lap and commenced to playing a game of tug-o'-war on the floor in front of the TV, using an athletic sock that he had found somewhere, probably under my sofa. Archie growled, shoulders hunched around his apple-shaped head, and Tommy mimicked him, showing his baby teeth as he grred.

Eunice began to nod, clearly connecting to whatever Felicia was saying. Vernon asked if I had anything to drink. I offered to make some coffee. He asked if I had anything stronger, so I handed him my last Budweiser.

"Part of it's my fault," he said, more mellow after a few swallows. "I took away her TV."

"Why?"

"All those damn infomercials. And that goddamned QVC channel, forget about it! I walk in one morning and there's five Cuisinarts on the kitchen counter and an Ionic Breeze in every room, including the plug-in models for the john."

"Maybe she needs a more supervised environment," I said.

"You offering?"

"I didn't encourage this," I said, a bit defensively. "I tried to put the kibosh on it, but the more I tried, the more stubborn she became."

"I go by every day," he said. "Or every other day, to make sure she's taking her meds and there's food in the house."

"What about her car keys?"

"Took them once and she went on a hunger strike."

"I guess I'm lucky that way," I said. "To be spared that. My mom died last year."

"You're lucky that your mom died."

"I meant the role reversal. I don't know how good a parent I would have been to her."

"Well, my own kids won't talk to me, so if I live to be her age, I'm screwed."

He was finished with his beer, Felicia was finished with her speech, and Eunice, I guessed, was finished with her recalcitrance. She allowed Felicia to help her rise from the sofa. I fetched the tote.

Vernon said, "Hide that damned thing."

"I will follow you home," Eunice said to Vernon.

"No, Momma, I'll drive. We'll pick up your car later."

"I am a burden to you," she said.

"No, Momma."

"It is a terrible thing," Eunice announced from the doorway. "All this . . ." waving her hand in my general direction, but I got the idea she was getting at something much bigger.

And then they were gone, and I stood in the middle of the room, clutching the tote.

"If you threw that into a fire," Felicia said, "would you burn up, too?"

She turned toward Tommy and Archie, still frolicking on the floor.

"Come on, kiddo," she called. "We're late for dinner."

"Hey," I said. "Thanks. For everything."

"Do you really think I have pleasant knees?"

"You bet." I was blushing.

"That's sweet . . . and weird—what's her name?"

"Amanda."

"Not your type, Ruzak."

"She *is* a little moribund."

"Pushy. I see you with some sweet, naïve thing, a type-B personality."

She took a deep breath, steeling herself, and called again to Tommy. He ignored her. She looked at me. I walked over and scooped up the dog. Tommy's pudgy arms shot up and he hopped up and down, trying to wrest the animal from my grip. Felicia grabbed his wrist.

"Say good-bye to Archie," she said. "If you're good, Ruzak might bring him over for another visit."

"You bet," I said. "That's a promise."

Tommy burst into tears. I was sure Felicia had set him up for this good-bye, had told him Archie was Ruzak's dog, not his, and every hello implied a good-bye. But the kid looked shocked, as if leaving Archie behind was the last thing he expected. I communicated my question to Felicia with my eyes—*Why not?*—and she shook her head angrily. She pulled Tommy toward the door, as he reached for the animal in my arms with his free hand, his face scarlet and glistening.

"Hate Roo-zack!" he hollered. "I *hate Roo-Zack!*"

There was no comforting him, so I tried to comfort Archie as he whined and scratched at my forearms to join Tommy.

"I'll call you later," Felicia shouted over the ruckus. "And congratulations!"

"For what?"

"For nabbing the killer!"

The door slammed and, after that, the silence. I was alone again, except for Archie, who leapt from my arms and scratched frantically at the door, going up on his hind legs and pawing at the wood just below the doorknob.

Later that long night, as Archie, exhausted, lay curled in front of the door, waiting for his boy to return, I pulled a random page from Eunice's manuscript and read this:

> *You would think living alone would free me from all the normal burdens of responsibility that people complain or worry about, but all living alone does is increase your psychological weight, as if your soul were living on Jupiter. It tends to make you more important to yourself and exaggerate your problems to the point that they're insurmountable afflictions.*

The passage got my heart rate up. Not only did it strike me as eerily prescient, it even sounded like something I would say. Either Eunice Shriver had found her way into my head or I had indeed found my way into hers.

DECEMBER 7

THIRTY-SIX

I had trouble falling asleep—go figure—so the phone ringing at two A.M. broke only the lightest of dozes. I noted two things before answering: Archie's staring from the bedroom doorway and the display on my cordless, UNKNOWN CALLER.

"Hello?" Silence answered, but for a slight background hissing. It might have been someone breathing; it might not. "You keep calling, but you won't say anything," I said. "Like God." Maybe that's it. Maybe that was as far as he would reach. I chased that thought away. Time to get focused. "I'm going out on a limb here, but I'm guessing you're connected in some way to the murder of Jack Minor. That's his name—he had a name, you know; he wasn't just some faceless vagrant, some useless parasite. He was a man, a human being like you and me.

"Maybe you know what happened, maybe you were involved or know who was involved, but you should know a man is sitting in jail for the murder, and you and I both know he isn't guilty. He's there because he thinks it's the safest place to be right now, and he's left it up to me to save him. That's ironic, since he wouldn't be sitting there right now if he hadn't put his trust in me.

I heard a sound like a sigh, pitched in an upper register, like a child's . . . or a woman's.

"I'll double the reward," I offered. "Fifty thousand dollars."

No answer. I looked at Archie, his big brown eyes shining in the ambient light coming from the bathroom. For almost thirty-four years, I had slept with a light on. I had read somewhere that God is to us as we are to dogs, that the gulf separating our intellects must be, if God is God, wider than the universe. Archie sensed I cared for him. He sensed his entire existence relied upon my tender feelings. But my thoughts were unfathomable, unknowable, and so he stared, unable to reach me except through signals as easily interpretable to me as mine were ineffable to him.

"You know," I said into the phone. "This is a little like praying. I talk and hope you are listening, and I don't expect a reply. At least, not a direct one. Look, I can't help you and you can't help me—or yourself—unless you tell me what you want. What do you want?"

Silence.

"One way or the other, I'll find you," I said, but the promise sounded hollow in my own ears. "I won't stop till I do, so why don't you make it easy for both of us? It's the *why* more than anything. I got the *what* and the *when* and the *where*. I even have the *who,* sort of. The *why* is what I'm getting at. You don't have to tell me who. Tell me why. Why is Jack dead? Why was God's hidden name carved on his forehead?"

A tiny voice whispered, a girl's voice, "He'll kill me."

I started to ask Who? but that would break my promise not five seconds after I made it. There should be more lag time between a promise and its breaking.

"There's gotta be a way we can do this," I said. I worked furiously at it, while Archie rested his chin between his forelegs, watching me.

"You don't have to actually tell me," I said. "I'll just ask a question and all you have to say is 'yes' or 'no.' How's that?"

That offer met with a long sigh. I couldn't tell if it was an acquiescent sigh or not.

"Do you know who killed Jack Minor?" I asked.

"Yes," came the answer, escaping from the receiver like air leaking from a tire.

"It wasn't another homeless man who killed him, was it?"

"No."

"There were three of them," I said.

"Yes."

"Students at UT?"

"Yes."

"Okay," I said. "Okay." I swung my legs out of the bed and ran a hand through my hair. Archie moved when I moved, sitting up, eyes locking onto me, lowering his nose toward the carpet.

"Were you there?" I asked.

"No."

"But you heard about it?"

"Yes."

I stood up. Archie rose with me. I shivered in my boxers. I felt larger somehow, or maybe the room just felt smaller.

"You weren't there, but somebody told you about it."

"Yes."

"And they made you promise not to tell anyone."

"Yes."

"Or they would hurt you?"

"No. Yes." I heard something on the other end that might have been a sob.

"It's going to be okay. You're doing the right thing. Don't be afraid."

"Yes."

"Doing the right thing is hardly ever easy. Otherwise, there'd be more right things being done. One thing you gotta keep to the forefront is the fact that keeping vital information from the police about a crime is also a crime."

"Yes."

"I can help you," I said. I wasn't sure I could, really, but these crumbs she was dropping marked the only path toward justice.

"Tomorrow I'm getting a list of names of students. If I showed you that list, could you highlight a name or two for me?"

I waited for her answer. Archie padded to the edge of the bed and sat down about a foot from my cold feet. He looked up at me.

She didn't answer. I went on. "Tomorrow night, eight o'clock at World's Fair Park, at the base of the Sunsphere. Look for the guy in the floppy brown hat. Can you do that? Can you do that for me? Can you do that for Jack?"

Archie and I waited for the answer.

THIRTY-SEVEN

The phone rang again at eight-thirty, snapping me out of a restless sleep.

"Yep," I said instead of "hello."

"Ruzak?"

"Oh, yeah."

It was Felicia, raising her voice to be heard over Tommy's wails in the background.

"Tommy wants to talk to the dog."

"Right now?"

"And then I want to talk to you."

Archie still manned his station by the bedroom door. I whistled, snapped my fingers and called his name, but he remained in his sphinxlike pose.

"I'm thinking I might remind him of his former owner," I said. "And it wasn't a happy relationship."

I held the receiver by the dog's ear while Tommy brayed on the line. The tip of Archie's tail twitched, and the end of his tongue swiped over his nose.

Felicia came back on the line.

"I'm meeting you for breakfast," she said.

"You are?"

"You have other plans?"

I admitted that, as usual, I was planless. An hour later, we were sitting in a booth at Pete's Diner. Felicia was wearing a chartreuse turtleneck, a long black skirt, and matching black boots. The day was overcast, with snow likely in the afternoon.

"Reggie Matthews is innocent," I said after the waitress left to turn in our order. Western omelet for me, a bagel and fruit cup for her. I told her about my conversation with Unknown Caller.

"Could be a prank," she said. "Some college kid sees your flyer and decides to have a laugh at your expense."

"It'd be hard to think of a sicker joke," I said.

"They didn't actually offer you any information, Ruzak."

"No, but she did offer *con*firmation."

"You're about to lay a hypo on me, aren't you?"

"One of the guys who did this told his girlfriend, swore her to secrecy and, I think, threatened her to keep her mouth shut. But it's been weighing on her conscience, and one day she sees my number on the flyer—"

"Or she sees the dollar sign on the flyer."

"Could be a little of both, but you shouldn't always assign the worst motives to people."

"What if the boyfriend's setting you up? He knows you're poking around and this was his way of finding out what you know. Then you, being the crackerjack detective that you are, set up a clandestine meeting in a dark, deserted place—"

"I'll bring my gun."

She pushed her plate a few inches toward me and folded her arms on the tabletop, leaning forward slightly, so I got a whiff of White Diamonds by Liz Taylor.

"Now about this dog, Ruzak. Some things in life are impossible. Sometimes those things are the things you want the most. And the sooner you develop your own personal solution to that dilemma, between the wanting and the can't-having, the better off you'll be."

"You're teaching Tommy a lesson? Why can't he have the dog?"

"Bob's allergic."

"Oh."

"Don't do that. Don't say 'oh' like that."

"It's just an 'oh.'"

"Nothing is just what it is with you."

"I guess you're saying I never learned the lesson you're trying to teach Tommy."

"I guess I'm saying exactly what I'm saying. It's incredibly hard for me to imagine a scenario in which your mentioning my knees has any meaningful context."

"It might have been a non sequitur. You know I have that problem."

"What problem?"

"With linear thought."

"Ruzak, what goes on in your head never bothered me much. It's part of what makes Ruzak, Ruzak. It's what's going on in your heart that's bothering me."

It hit me, finally, what she was getting at.

"I don't have a crush," I protested. "I really don't. I was dealing with a high-pressure situation. She's not subtle, this girl, and it was a desperate moment."

"You could have brought up your old girlfriend from high school," Felicia pointed out. She reached up with her left hand and tucked a strand of her hair behind her ear.

"She's married. To a guy named Bill Hill."

"So would Amanda know that?"

"It's been more than a couple years since high school. What kind of guy carries a torch for sixteen years?"

"Oh, Ruzak, and I always took you for a romantic."

"Again, my only defense is you're the one woman I know who's around my age and around *me*—"

"A random choice?" She was smiling.

"Sure. No. I mean, I don't really know why I brought up your knees. I'll never do it again. It's not as if I said you had ugly knees. Pleasant and well formed, I think I said, and that part wasn't a lie. I've admired your knees for some time now, though I'm no voyeur or pervert; I mean, I don't have a knee fetish or anything like that, though I'm sure there's men—and women— who do; you can have a fetish on practically anything. Well, not practically. *Literally.* Anyway, it's been my experience—or observation, I guess I should say—that a lot of women don't have any kind of knee structure to brag about, not even those fashion models, whose knees tend toward knobbiness, very unattractive," I said rapidly, and sipped my cold coffee.

"Bring the cops along," Felicia said.

"What?"

"To your rendezvous tomorrow night. That way, they can bust whoever shows up: the girl as a material witness or the perp as the . . . well, the perp."

"I'll call Detective Black."

"You could have used her as your excuse."

"She has a mean smile."

Felicia laughed. "What about her knees?"

"I never looked, to be honest."

"What do you suppose that means? That you took the time to notice mine but not hers?"

I looked right into her eyes and said, "I don't ascribe any meaning to it at all."

THIRTY-EIGHT

Of course, she could have pointed out, correctly, that that was my biggest problem: I ascribed meaning to everything, even to things that had no meaning or no potential meaning, like the letters on Jack Minor's forehead, or that my concern for life (the ferns) that brought me to the office the morning after Jack's murder had anything to do with my finding him. Life is pretty damned random, and maybe it was the randomness that terrified me.

I called Detective Black the minute I got back to the apartment, the omelet resting uneasily in my gut. I distrusted my digestive powers. Growing up, I was always the nauseated kid, puking in the school bathroom before the big test.

"What if I told you I've turned up a corroborating witness?" I asked her.

"A corroborating witness to what?"

"Reggie's story."

"Which one, the one he told you or the one he told us?"

"The first one."

"The one about the three college kids who committed murder just for the heck of it?"

"Right. That one." I filled her in on Unknown Caller. "I'm meeting her tomorrow night at World's Fair Park."

"Well, let me know how that goes."

"You don't want in on it?"

"I would definitely want in on it if there was anything to be in on."

"Don't you think that might make the being in on it difficult if you're not there?"

"I appreciate the offer, Mr. Ruzak, but at this point we're satisfied we're in on the only story that matters."

"How come?"

"Because nobody in Reggie's position would confess to something he didn't do, Mr. Ruzak." It was taking some effort, I could tell, for her to remain civil.

"That's exactly why he confessed," I said.

"Why is exactly why?"

"His position. He doesn't trust his son to keep him safe—it wasn't hard for even someone like me to find him. And he didn't trust me to keep him safe. So he confesses to you, knowing you'll lock him up, which gives me time to find the real killers."

"Wow. That's a heck of a theory. A man risks life in prison because he's afraid he might lose his life out of prison."

She was right: It *was* a heck of a theory, but no theory is perfect. Look at all the holes in Darwin's.

"He's hunkered," I said. "He figures he might as well hunker in jail where he'll be safe while he waits for this to play out. He can recant at any time, and then what do you have? There's nothing else tying him to the crime."

"You think he's that smart?"

"Just because you're a semisuicidal homeless alcoholic doesn't mean you're not smart." I didn't tell her I had sort of planted the seed of this idea. She might perceive it as bragging.

DECEMBER 8

THIRTY-NINE

*W*orld's Fair Park, situated between the University of Tennessee campus and downtown Knoxville, was built in 1982. There's a pavilion and an amphitheater set amid acres of rolling green park. The nearly three-hundred-foot-tall Sunsphere near the center of the original park dominates the landscape downtown, with its shiny gold dome sitting atop its Eiffel-Tower-like scaffolding. For years there was a restaurant at the top, but they closed it down; I'm not sure why.

At seven-forty, I was standing at the base of the sphere, wearing my mustard-stained floppy hat and my trench coat, both hands stuffed into the pockets. In the left was Professor Heifitz's class roster. In the right, the .45-caliber gun I bought from Wal-Mart, back when I naïvely thought I had a fighting chance to become a real detective, before I flunked the PI exam, before the state shut me down for flunking, before I found Jack Minor's mutilated corpse in the alley when all I wanted to accomplish that day was rescue some ferns.

I could hear the traffic along Cumberland Avenue, the main drag through campus, and see the flickering headlamps of the cars on the interstate. To the west, I guessed from the apartments across the street from the museum, a dog barked, a clipped, hard-edged sound in the frigid air.

At a quarter after eight, she still hadn't shown. I decided to give her another ten minutes. It couldn't have been more than a couple minutes later when the first blow landed between my shoulder blades. I stayed on my feet, stumbling forward a couple of steps. Behind me, I heard the scraping of shoes against concrete. The second blow landed in the lower back, a kidney punch that dropped me to my knees. My hands came out when I went down, to brace my fall. Kneeling, I fumbled in my pocket for the gun, and took the next blow at the base of the skull. I pitched forward, meeting the concrete with my nose. I heard a *crunch* and tasted blood rising from the back of my throat. Much warmer than the surrounding air, the blood steamed as it hit the pavement, pouring from my broken nose.

A hand grabbed my right wrist and yanked it up to the base of my neck. I howled. A knee pressed into the small of my back and I felt the warmth of someone's breath in my ear.

"You want to be next?" a male voice hissed. "That what you want, motherfucker?"

The fingers of his free hand dug into my hair and yanked my head back. I swallowed a wad of blood and snot.

"Don't fuck with us, Ruzak. We know where you live."

He shoved my face straight down. I managed to twist my head just in time, so my left cheekbone hit first and not my smashed nose. All I accomplished with that maneuver, though, was a smashed cheekbone.

He released me. I pushed myself up. Then he kicked me in the ribs, and the toe of his shoe wasn't soft, like a sneaker, but hard, like a reinforced work boot or steel-plated cowboy boot.

I flopped back down, gun completely forgotten, clutching my side. I suspected he'd broken a rib.

"Stay down, Ruzak," he said softly.

I took a few deep breaths and pushed myself back up. He kicked me again, twice, taking care to hit me in the same spot, where he could cause the most pain.

"What the hell is the matter with you? Stay *down*."

I started to get back up. He snorted with frustration, a kind of hiccuping laugh, and let me have it again, until I heard another crunching sound and felt a stabbing pain deep inside my chest. I wondered if a rib had punctured my lung. My vision was clouding, but I tried to get up.

"Moron," he said, and commenced to kick again. My legs

moved against the ground, propelling me forward, like a Marine in an obstacle course. He must have kept pace beside me, because he managed to land his kicks in the same spot each time.

"Give up, why doncha? Why doncha just give up?"

One last time I tried to rise. He wasn't expecting it and missed the spot in my side, hitting instead my solar plexus. I collapsed, writhing and gasping for air, but hung onto consciousness long enough to hear his last words before darkness overwhelmed me.

"Nice hat," he said.

FORTY

I had a very odd dream in which I was a dog. I'm assuming I was Archie, because I was sitting on my kitchen floor watching my human self peel a carrot. As I stared, the carrot began to squirm and wriggle, growing fatter and longer until it morphed into a rattlesnake as thick as my arm. I kept working as the snake whipped about, peeling off the skin, long glistening strands of it falling into the sink as its blood ran down my forearms. The snake's mouth came open, revealing three-inch fangs. The human-me just kept peeling. The dog-me barked.

I woke up in a hospital bed, an IV line snaking from my arm. Someone stirred in the chair beside me, rose, and came to stand beside the bed. I smelled White Diamonds.

"Hi, Ruzak," Felicia said. "How do you feel?"

"Floaty."

"You have Demerol in your drip."

"Oh. It's pretty good stuff. . . . How bad is it?"

"Not too bad. A fractured rib, a broken nose, a few lacerations here and there. You'll live."

I eased my hand to my face and touched the bandages over my nose.

"I was bushwhacked," I said.

Her eyes seemed very large in the subdued lighting of the hospital room. She had pulled her hair back, but I couldn't tell if it was in a bun or a ponytail. As the year had grown old, Felicia's hair had grown darker. She had begun the year a Dolly Parton blonde. Now the color was nearing a Penelope Cruz brown.

"You were lucky," she said. "Lucky he didn't kill you and lucky we got to you as soon as we did. You might have gone into hypothermia."

"Got to me?"

"I figured you'd call me. So when I didn't hear from you, I called you. When I couldn't reach you, I called Bob—he's on duty tonight and the station's only about a half mile from the park."

"Bob found me?"

She nodded, smiling, and her nose crinkled in the middle.

"You said you wanted to meet him, remember?"

"He didn't have to do anything like mouth-to-mouth, did he?"

She laughed and shook her head. "If he did, he didn't tell me about it."

"Would he?"

She laughed again. "Anyway, I didn't want you to wake up by your lonesome."

She laid her hand on my forearm, just below the IV. Her hand was cold.

"Did you get a good look at him?" she asked.

"No. He jumped me from behind."

"Well, it's a helluva price to pay, Ruzak, but at least now we know you were right about Reggie."

At that moment, the door swung open and Detective Black strode into the room. Felicia removed her hand from my arm.

"Well, Mr. Ruzak," Detective Black said. Her nose was bright red and the color was high in her cheeks.

"I was right about Reggie," I told her.

She showed me her teeth in what I took for Meredith Black's version of a noncommittal smile.

"Hello," she said, turning to Felicia. "I'm Detective Meredith Black with the Knoxville PD."

"This is Felicia, my secretary. Well, technically, my former secretary."

"Girl Friday and dog-sitter," Felicia corrected me.

"Oh," Meredith said. "Nice." She turned back to me. "Feel up to giving me a statement?"

"I better go," Felicia said.

"Okay." Meredith smiled in her general direction.

"Why don't you stay?" I asked. I looked at Meredith. "I got an armful of Demerol and I have trouble organizing my thoughts in the best of circumstances."

"I don't understand," Meredith said.

"I think Teddy wants me to stick around, as a kind of interpreter," Felicia said.

"He seems lucid to me."

"Appearances can be deceiving," Felicia said. "I used to think he was pretty smart."

"It really doesn't matter to me," Meredith said. She slipped into the chair Felicia had vacated and dug a tape recorder from her purse. It was a very large, tote-sized purse.

"Here's the deal," I began, and brought the Knoxville PD up to snuff. Felicia hung by the door, arms folded over her chest. If Bob was working, I wondered, where was Tommy? And what about my dog?

"So I guess this girl was a no-show," Meredith said.

"I don't know. I didn't see her, but that doesn't necessarily mean she wasn't there."

"And she didn't give you a name over the phone?"

"If she had given me a name over the phone, I wouldn't have set up the meeting in the park."

"Seems an awfully convoluted way to go about it," Meredith observed. "And risky. Luring you to a public place like that. Why not jump you in the parking lot under the Sterchi?"

"Well, I really can't answer that," I answered. "I'm not in his head."

"My point is, why would they arrange something so elaborate and risky just to send you a message to back off? All these calls basically an act to lure you over there tonight? It doesn't make sense."

"Not much has since I found him," I said, meaning Jack.

"I'm just wondering if there's an element to this you've left out."

"I don't think so. . . ."

"You're asking me to believe that the three people involved in this crime, if there were three people, involved a fourth person in their conspiracy to commit an act that blows any chance they have of getting off scot-free."

I thought about what she said. Then I asked, "Huh?"

"Reggie's confession was reported in the newspaper. Odds are they know somebody's taking the fall for them. Why would they do something which sends the message we got the wrong guy?"

"I don't know. All I know is my nose is broken."

"Maybe this has nothing to do with the death of Jack Minor," Meredith Black said.

"How couldn't it?"

"I think only you could answer that question, Mr. Ruzak."

From across the room, Felicia exploded.

"Oh, Jesus Christ, I'm not believing this! He's had the living shit beat out of him; he might have frozen to death out there tonight; and you're sitting there accusing him of lying about the whole thing! Where do you people get off? Ruzak's got a lot of problems, God knows, but one of them isn't dishonesty. He's the most honest person I've ever known."

"It isn't a matter of Mr. Ruzak's honesty," Meredith snapped back. "It's a matter of consistency and logic."

"Well," I said. "Those two things do happen to be problems."

"Shut up, Ruzak," Felicia said. "Why are you giving in to this . . ." She started to call her a name, then backed off. ". . . person?" She turned back to Meredith. "It is consistent and it is logical. I don't think it was a setup. Or it didn't become a setup until after the last phone call. I think she's a girlfriend of one of these guys. He told her about Jack, then one day she sees Ruzak's poster on campus. She starts calling him, but she can't bring herself to say anything until yesterday."

"Why?" Meredith asked. Her tone was sharp, but she was smiling, ever the biter.

"Why the hell does *why* matter? Maybe she really loves the guy and doesn't want to see him go to jail for the rest of his life. Maybe she's scared—she told Ruzak he would kill her—maybe she's both, in love and scared, and then she finds out an innocent man is going to pay for something her boyfriend did and that finally makes her talk.

"Look, this isn't brain surgery. All you have to do now is take that list and go through the names. Because his name is on that list. His or one of the other's or maybe all three. There's no other reason he'd do this. You wanted to know why he risked it—that's why."

"It isn't a long list," I said. "Twenty-seven names, twenty of which are male."

"Don't make us do it," Felicia said to Meredith.

"Excuse me?"

"Don't make me and Ruzak go down that list. Can you imagine what the *Sentinel* would do with that story, how the Knoxville PD sat on its ass while some boneheaded loser PI who isn't even a PI caught the real killers?"

Meredith looked down at my broken face. I said, "She never wanted me involved in this." The remark about the boneheaded loser PI stung, but I knew Felicia was just driving home a point.

DECEMBER 9

FORTY-ONE

*M*y breakfast the next morning was surprisingly good for a hospital. Eggs, toast, two pancakes, and a glass of orange juice. I asked the lady who brought the food when I could go home, and she said as soon as the doctor cleared me. So I ate my breakfast and waited for the doctor. I studied the IV in my arm and worried about a staph infection; a hospital really is the worst place to be sick: The longer you stay, the higher your odds of getting seriously ill from something that had nothing to do with your being there.

Felicia called to check on me.

"I don't know when I can leave," I said to her, half complaining, half explaining.

"Can you get a ride home?" she asked, which I took to mean

she couldn't be that ride. Probably something to do with Tommy, or Bob, or both—or neither. There were whole areas of Felicia's life that I knew nothing about.

"I'll figure something out," I said. "You probably saved my life last night, and I don't think I thanked you."

"Was that a thanks?"

"More of a lead-in. Thank you. And make sure you thank Bob for me."

"It couldn't have worked out better," Felicia said. She sounded tired, and I wondered how much sleep she had gotten the night before. "Now that our pal Meredith has the list."

"What if the list proves to be a dead end?"

"Ruzak, at some point you have to say enough."

"Maybe I shouldn't, though, as long as Reggie's behind bars."

"You have more important things to do, like studying for your PI exam."

"Right. Um."

"'Right um'?"

"Well, sometimes circumstances force you to look at things with a fresh eye."

"Meaning?"

"Meaning maybe detective work and I aren't a good fit."

"If you really mean that, why are you thinking about doing more with this case?"

"I'm not sure how much that has to do with me being a detective."

"Oh, Christ. You're so . . ."

"Boneheaded?"

"You're sore about that."

"A little."

"I was trying to make a point, that's all."

"That's what I figured."

"It has its advantages, you know. Being a bonehead."

"Name one."

The silence that ensued weighed on us both. Finally, I said, "I'm worried about Archie."

"Archie's fine. I swung by your apartment on the way home and picked him up."

"How'd you get in?"

"I took your keys."

"So how will I get in?"

"Turn the knob. I didn't lock it. Your keys are on the kitchen counter."

"So Archie's with you?"

"Until you come by and get him. And the sooner, the better, Ruzak."

There weren't too many names on my list of people I could count on to give me a ride. I called the Humane Society.

"I'm in the hospital," I told Amanda.

"What happened?"

"A bad guy jumped me."

"Oh, my God! Are you okay?"

"Well, the doctor just came through and said I could go home."

"Did they catch the guy?"

"Not yet, but they have his name."

"What is it?"

"I don't know."

"You just said they had his name."

"They have his name on a list."

"Dear Jesus, how many people attacked you?"

"It's kind of a long story. The reason I'm calling is I need a lift back to my apartment."

"My shift doesn't end till three."

"Oh. Well, maybe I'll call a cab, then. I think they need the room."

"No, no, don't do that. I'll make a couple of calls. Give me an hour, okay? I'll be there."

"Okay."

I decided to get dressed and hit the john before she arrived. The last thing I wanted—well, not the last in the absolute sense—was her to see me in a hospital gown. I had trouble buttoning my shirt over the bandages protecting my ribs, and pulling up my pants proved a challenge of physical engineering. I hurt like hell after it was over, and double-checked my wallet for the subscription for painkillers the attending physician had written. I was surprised to find my gun in the pocket of my overcoat. You would think a hospital would have tighter security procedures.

I avoided my reflection in the bathroom mirror, but the little glances I shot that way were not encouraging. Both eyes had shiners, giving me a raccoonlike appearance. I wondered if my nose would come out crooked after the bandages came off, and what that would do to my overall appearance. Might it give my otherwise bland features some character? Well, I thought, at least my basic optimism is still intact.

I sat in the chair by the bed and tried to gather my thoughts, though the effects of the Demerol still lingered. A thought would dash across my mind and I would chase after it, like Alice after the rabbit, until it hopped down my cerebral hole and was gone.

There could be only one reason I was jumped the night before. Like Meredith said, it was a huge risk, and the only thing that made the risk worth taking was a name on the list I promised Unknown Caller I had. At some point, from the time I set up the rendezvous and last night, this guy found out about me and the list and decided he didn't have a choice but to try to warn me off the case.

I had accomplished that, at least: narrowing his options. That spawned another half-formed thought, or more of an emotion struggling to become a thought, and that emotion felt a lot like fear.

I was still chasing rabbits when Amanda walked into the room, took one look at my smashed-up face, and brought a hand to her mouth.

"It looks worse than it feels," I told her.

"Lean on me," she said.

"The doctor says I might need to use a cane for a few weeks."

"This has something to do with the dead guy in the alley, doesn't it?"

I nodded. "He's running out of options," I said. During the elevator ride and the long, slow walk to the parking lot, with my big self draped over her skinny frame, I told her about the list and Unknown Caller.

"And now I've got a bad feeling," I said, as she helped me lower myself into the passenger seat of the Monte Carlo.

"I bet you do," she said.

I shifted in my seat as she drove, trying to find a comfortable position. That had been a problem of mine for some time. I said, "I mean, about her. He can't trust her now."

"You think he'll hurt her?"

"I'm just wondering if the reason I didn't see her last night was because she wouldn't come, or if it was because she *couldn't* come."

"Oh, God."

"But it's one of those things where there's nothing you can do. I've been faced with that a lot lately. From Jack in that alley to Eunice Shriver, even to Archie, with all that angst-ridden staring."

"I don't think dogs suffer from angst, Ruzak."

"Well. The point is, fear is a very useful emotion. We're capable of it for a reason. It's supposed to spur us to action, the flight-or-flight thing, but I've got nothing to fight and nothing to fly from, really. There's no way to find her. All I can do is pray she's safe."

"Maybe she'll call again."

"I doubt it. She's afraid, too. She was afraid before, obviously, but now she's very afraid. Now she's terrified."

I asked her to swing through the Buddy's Barbeque drive-thru on Kingston Pike; I was starving. I had a pulled-pork sandwich and side of coleslaw. Amanda ordered a hot-fudge cake.

"I live on these things," she confided.

"Don't you worry about things like proper nutrition, saturated fat content, and stuff like that?"

"No more than you," she said, eying my sandwich.

In the lobby of the Sterchi, we passed a man whose name I knew only as Whittaker. Whittaker was the assistant apartment manager.

"Ruzak?" he asked.

"I had a little accident," I said.

"Looks slightly larger than little. I need to talk to you. I got a report that you've violated your lease."

"How so?"

"You're aware we're a pet-free facility?"

"I think I remember something about that."

"We've had reports, Mr. Ruzak."

"Look, he's been seriously injured," Amanda said. "He needs to get off his feet."

Whittaker ignored her. "Are you denying you've taken a dog into this building?"

"I was affirming that I knew I couldn't keep a pet."

"Are you?"

"I just did."

"No, are you denying you have a dog?" he asked, his voice rising.

"I do not currently have a dog, no," I said carefully.

Amanda edged us toward the elevator. Whittaker trailed behind, hot on the scent.

"You do know, as the assistant manager of this facility, that I have the right to enter your apartment at any time to conduct an inspection of compliance with your lease agreement?"

"I wasn't specifically aware of that, but I'll take your word for it."

"I'll be happy to supply you with a copy," Whittaker said. "We take enforcement very seriously here at the Sterchi, Mr. Ruzak."

"Oh, I'm a firm believer in enforcement," I replied. "But as of this moment, I don't have a dog."

The elevator doors slid closed, and we left Mr. Something Whittaker or Mr. Whittaker Something behind.

"You got rid of Arch?" Amanda asked.

"Felicia took him. But I have to get him back."

"Felicia of the pleasant knees."

She walked me to the sofa.

"Comfy?" she asked.

"Not really."

"Maybe you should lie down in the bed."

"I'll get used to it."

"We should have got you a cane. Or a walker, like old ladies use."

I asked her to fetch me the cordless. There were no new calls and no messages.

"Seriously, Ruzak, tell me what else you need."

"I did forget this," I said, showing her the prescription.

"I'll go get it filled," she said, snatching it from my hand.

"You don't need to do that."

"It's no big deal," she said, and headed for the door. "There's a Walgreens right on Gay Street."

Then she was gone. I sat on my sofa and thought I'd never seen her so animated. Sometimes all we need to feel alive is to feel useful.

After fifteen minutes of me staring at the TV remote lying on the coffee table, trying to work up the energy to get up and grab it, the phone rang. The number that popped up looked familiar, but I couldn't place it.

"Ruzak!" Vernon Shriver barked at me. "Where is my mother?"

"I haven't seen her," I said. "I just got home from the hospital."

"Why were you in the hospital?"

"Somebody beat me up."

"That don't surprise me. Well, she isn't home and she isn't here and she isn't at the church. What do you think?"

I told him I had no idea what I thought, but promised to call if I heard from her. He called me a name and hung up.

Another forty-five minutes went by, and still no sign of Amanda.

I wondered if Walgreens was giving her a hard time about the prescription because, obviously, she didn't look like somebody whose name could be Theodore Ruzak.

Felicia called to ask if I got home okay.

"Did you take a cab?" she asked.

"No," I said. "I took Amanda. I mean, Amanda gave me a ride. I mean, she drove me home."

"Amanda," she said. "Well, you know what this means."

"What?"

"She's got a real thing for you, Ruzak. I just don't understand your reluctance."

"I'm not the any-port-in-a-storm kind of guy."

"It's her knees, isn't it?"

"They do have a certain knobby quality."

Another half hour went by before Amanda finally returned, the white paper Walgreens' drug sack in one hand and a small duffel in the other.

"What now?" I asked.

"I decided to run by my place and grab a few things. You're gonna need some help until you get back on your feet."

"You're moving in?"

"Just for a few days. Is that a problem?"

I sat very still, trying to think of one way in which it might be. She laughed.

"Don't worry, Ruzak. You're in no condition to hanky-panky, even if you wanted to. I'll bunk out here on the sofa."

She dropped her duffel to the floor and commenced to rummaging through my pantry. She was wearing stretchy black pants that accentuated her glutes as she bent over.

"You must eat out a lot," she called over her shoulder. She leaned on the kitchen counter, unwrapping a Twinkie. I wasn't sure, but it may have been my last Twinkie.

"There's no tree," she said, looking around. "Don't you celebrate Christmas?"

"I used to put up a tree for Mom," I said. "This is my first Christmas without her."

"Maybe that's the problem," Amanda said. "A Freudian element."

"I'd hate to think so."

"All I'm saying is, maybe older women turn you on."

"Well," I said. "I watch a lot of old movies, and I always had a thing for Sophia Loren."

"Oh God, Ruzak, she's nearly as old as Eunice Shriver."

"I think that's why I've been so indulgent," I said. "Not because of Sophia Loren, but because Eunice showed up right after my mom died."

"Do you do that a lot?" she asked, finishing off the Twinkie and licking the white cream from her fingertips. What the hell was in that cream, anyway? "All the navel gazing?"

"More than I should," I admitted. "Probably I'm trying to keep the cosmic scales balanced against the people who should, but don't."

DECEMBER 20

FORTY-TWO

My first impression of Reggie Matthews through the bullet-proof pane was how much better his looks had improved since his incarceration: neatly shaved, his hair shorter and thicker looking, calm and well rested. More than poor diet or lack of exercise, it's fear and anxiety that tear our appearances apart. Reggie didn't have to worry anymore where his next meal was coming from, or if he'd find a warm place to sleep for the night. Or if he was doomed to suffer a useless, unjust death at the hands of a punk.

"Reggie," I said into the telephone receiver. "You look terrific."

"You don't. He really did a number on you, Ruzak."

"It's reached that point where it looks worse than it feels."

"That's the point to get to, all right."

"Reggie," I said. "They're finished with the list."

He wet his lips. "They caught 'em all?"

"They caught nobody. Reggie, the list didn't pan out. Every guy on it had an alibi or didn't fit the descriptions you gave."

"So?"

"So I told Detective Black it didn't change the fact that I was attacked by somebody who warned me off this case. That this girl calling me and that guy jumping me could only point to your innocence."

He nodded. "And what'd she say?"

"She said I'd make a terrific witness for the defense."

"Well, sure."

"Reggie, here's the bottom line: You're going to trial next month for a murder we both know you didn't commit. Now, the Knoxville PD is playing this close to the vest—Meredith won't say what she'll do—but my guess is they'll fold their hands if you recant now. They don't have anything of any substance except your confession."

"I ain't recanting, Ruzak."

"How about Johnson City?" I asked. "You must have felt reasonably safe there."

"Are you kidding me?" he said with a laugh. "You hear from my boy?"

I nodded. "I told him you were doing just fine, but he asked to talk to you and I had to lie."

"What'd you say?"

"I told him you were walking my dog. What're you going to do when he decides to drive down for a little visit? Or he picks up the paper and reads about your trial?"

"Did you give him that money?"

"I did."

"Then he don't have any reason to come down. He never wanted much to do with me, Ruzak, even when he was little. You wanna know somethin'? I'm feelin' the best I have in years. Even gone off my medicine. I got a whole month to let this thing work itself out."

"These kind of things don't just work themselves out, Reggie. Maybe you should factor this into your decision: she hasn't called me since the attack, and the list is a dead end."

His eyes narrowed at me. "So?"

"So there's nothing the police can do and, more important, there's nothing more I can do. The only option left is for you to recant."

"Not yet."

"I don't get it," I said. "What are you waiting for, Reggie? The police think they have Jack's killer, so they're not looking. I've got no leads, so I'm not looking. And I sincerely doubt these guys are going to waltz into the station and confess. You're betting the police will have to let you go if you recant at the eleventh hour, but you don't know that for sure. They still may take you to trial, and men have been sent to the death chamber on less in this state."

"Ah, come on, Ruzak, what's the matter with you? It's almost Christmas. Don't you believe in miracles?"

I gave up after that. He seemed awfully cocksure for somebody whose fate hung by a thread. I left the prison, hobbling across the parking lot, leaning on the cane Amanda had bought me, carved from hickory with a gold handle in the shape of a duck's head. Bunting hung from the lampposts, bronze horns on a green background with HAPPY HOLIDAYS written in red beneath them. Somebody had thrown a few strands of Christmas lights around the evergreens by the entrance, the kind with the fat, multicolored bulbs, which was the only kind of lights I could remember from childhood; I think my childhood predated the minilights.

The overcast sky was spitting a fitful snow, and I walked slowly to my car, planting my feet carefully on the slick pavement. To the west, on the other side of the river, seven-foot-tall Christmas trees, red, green and white, glimmered on the roof of the First Tennessee Bank building, the tallest structure downtown.

I leaned the cane against the passenger seat and started the car. I felt heavy, weighed down. Foolish, too, to put so much stock into the list from Professor Heifitz. I wasn't attacked because a name was on a list; I was attacked because he must have found out she had talked to me and I deserved a stern warning.

It took over forty minutes on the Pike to get to West Town Mall and another ten to find a parking place, and that one tucked in the farthest corner. Driving was not a painless exercise, and

Amanda had offered to chauffer me, but I told her my independence was about all I had left. She seemed to understand. I had hoped that that would lead to a discussion about her moving out. It didn't.

I had lived alone for so long, her being in my apartment was both comforting and disconcerting. She was gone most of the day; the semester was over, but she had picked up more hours at the Humane Society. I discovered Amanda was a night owl. I'd wake up in the middle of the night to the sound of her raucous laughter on the phone, and she spent a lot of time on her laptop, crafting her MySpace. Archie enjoyed having her around, though. She was an old friend from his pound days, and it took his mind off whatever it was about me that troubled him.

Two days after I left the hospital, Vernon Shriver called me.

"We found her," he said without even saying hello.

"Where was she?"

"Hiding out at her preacher's house. I got her safe now. Put her in that home on Middlebrook Pike, you know the one?"

"I think I've heard of it. Wasn't that the one where the old guy killed himself a couple years back?"

"That's the one. Killed his wife, too. Think she had terminal cancer."

So Eunice Shriver was safely tucked away in a rest home, only they don't call them rest homes anymore for politically correct reasons that were hard for me to discern. Still, if anybody needed a rest, it was Eunice. I'd read somewhere that dementia wasn't a matter of *if* but *when*. You live long enough, you get it. Those ninety-year-olds with the minds sharp as tacks, they're doomed, too, if they beat the odds and make it another ten years. All the advances in medical science can't change the fact that the human body is designed to last for only so long. And still, in the twenty-first century, nobody can say for sure why we die, what makes our cells eventually stop doing what they're designed to do. Maybe this is the root cause of our sense of outrage and betrayal when the inevitable comes.

Felicia was waiting for me in the food court, wearing a red scarf and dangly ruby earrings, her hair pulled back into a cascade of blondness that fell to the middle of her back. She had colored her hair again. She smelled like cinnamon, though I might have been picking up the rolls from the Cinnabon place four tables away.

"Sorry," I said. "I couldn't find a spot."

"You should have used a handicapped one."

"I don't have a sticker."

"Ruzak, half the people parked in them don't, either, and half of those who do, shouldn't."

"Integrity begins as a personal issue," I said.

"You know, sometimes you say things that sound very smart but, if you really think about them, they kind of crumble apart like old cake."

She had taken the liberty of buying my lunch, a steaming steak-and-cheese from Charlie's Steakery. They served the fries, the greasiest I'd ever had, in a paper cup. Felicia had salad from McDonalds.

"Reggie won't recant," I told her.

"He's getting three squares a day and twenty-four-hour, tax-payer-provided protection. He figures he can wait till the last second and they'll have to let him go. Would you recant?"

"I wouldn't have confessed in the first place."

"Well," she said. "At least it's over and you can concentrate on more important things. Like passing your PI exam. Three weeks, Ruzak. You better be ready."

"I could let it go," I said. "If it weren't for her."

"Who her?"

"Unknown Caller. What if something happened to her? Why hasn't she called me?"

"Because it worked. He beat you up to send her a message, too."

"She said he would kill her."

"Has there been anything in the papers? Any story on TV? And even if he did do something to her, what're you going to do about it? She had the opportunity to be straight with you and she chose not to."

"One thing that puzzles me," I said. "Why did she call me and not the cops? That way she gets him locked up and unlocks up an innocent man."

"Maybe it's more than fear," Felicia said.

"She loves him?"

She shrugged. "It happens."

A frazzled-looking woman hurried by our table, arms loaded down with bags, two kids in tow as she talked on her cell phone.

"I haven't bought the first present," I told Felicia, watching the woman. "What does Tommy want?"

She gave me a look. "What do you think?"

"They do have hypoallergenic breeds."

"You know something? Whenever you say a word over four syllables there's this caressing thing that goes on with your mouth."

"Floccinaucinihilipilification."

"Flocci what?"

"It's the longest word in the *Oxford English Dictionary*."

"What does it mean?"

"The estimation that something is worthless."

"Like knowing the longest word in the *Oxford English Dictionary*. What was it again?"

"Floccinaucinihilipilification."

"Wow. That was practically orgasmic."

"Amanda asked me why I kept a dictionary in the bathroom."

"Do you think that's significant? That I say the word orgasmic and you think of Amanda?"

"Oh, nothing like that's going on. She sleeps on the sofa."

"Let me ask you something, Ruzak. Are you human?"

"She did ask me if I was gay. I told her I wasn't, but what if I am?"

"You're not gay, Ruzak."

"I've never been attracted to a man, but maybe that's only because I haven't been around the right man."

"I don't think the fact that you're not attracted to this girl means you're not attracted to girls. Does she still throw herself at you?"

"Once, the night she moved in, but that was more of a gentle toss."

"So when does she plan to move out? You're ambulatory now."

"I don't know how to broach the topic."

"How about, 'Hey, thanks for the help, but I'm okay now?'"

"I'm figuring it won't be long. She'll want to spend Christmas with her mom."

"So am I," Felicia said, pulling a compact out of her purse to check her face. Her red lips puckered at the mirror. "Not her mom, mine up in Kentucky."

"This'll be my first Christmas since Mom died," I said. "I'm thinking of spending it at the mission. The food wasn't all that bad at Thanksgiving, and it'll give me something to do."

"You need that," she said. "Something to do."

"The other thing I thought of was working the list myself. You know, maybe the cops missed something. I doubt they checked out all those guys' alibis. I've got a copy of it." I tapped my pocket. The idea had been to show the list to Reggie, but in the middle of our conversation it struck me how useless that would have been.

"You know what the secret to happiness is, Ruzak? Knowing when to give up."

I nodded. "That's it. You've hit it right on the money. Knowing which battles to fight and knowing the time to walk from the fray. But it's like great sex. Afterward, when the moment's done, there's the 'what next.' I don't have any what-next."

"You don't have the sex, either."

She dropped the compact into her purse and pulled out a small notebook. The tip of her tongue came out as she studied whatever was written in it.

"What is that?" I asked.

"Shopping list, Ruzak."

"I haven't bought the first present," I said.

"I know, you already told me."

"Do you ever worry about dementia?"

"Only when I'm with you."

"Eunice's son committed her to a rest home."

"They don't call them rest homes anymore, Ruzak."

"I know. Why is that?"

"Does it matter?"

"That's my other problem," I said. "One of my other problems. Figuring out what matters."

"Here's what matters," she said. "Knowing for certain I've taken care of everyone on the list."

She noticed me staring at her.

"What?"

"'Everyone on the list,'" I said.

"Even the mailman. He loves M&Ms, so I have to hit the Candy Factory before I leave."

"There were twenty-seven names on that seminar's class roster," I said. "Twenty of which are male. Felicia, Detective Black told me they interviewed every guy on that list. Every *guy* on that list."

I pulled the list from my pocket and showed her.

"They never talked to the girls," I said.

She let the notebook fall closed and said, "I'll drive."

FORTY-THREE

I made the calls from the passenger seat of Felicia's Corolla. The first and third were picked up by an automated voicemail system, and I hung up without leaving a message. We could always swing by the addresses later. The second, fourth, and fifth also went to voicemails, these with personalized greetings, but I didn't leave a message on those, either. I didn't want to spoil the element of surprise.

"School's out for the semester break," I said. "We might not get anybody."

The sixth call was answered on the tenth ring, right as I was about to hang up.

"Hello?"

I glanced at the list. Angela Cummings. "Angela," I said. "This is Teddy Ruzak."

A good ten seconds of silence, and then the line went dead.

I looked over at Felicia. "I think my network dropped the call."

Felicia started the car. "Bullshit," she said, and whipped out of the parking space. Then it took ten minutes just to get out of the lot and onto Kingston Pike, where the brake lights twinkled very Christmaslike. Felicia banged her palm of the steering wheel.

"Damn, damn, *damn*," she said.

"You should cut over on Papermill to the interstate," I said.

"Really, you think? Thank you *so* much, Ruzak, for stating the obvious! Why do you men do that?"

"Here's my theory—"

"Screw your theories! You have more theories than China has people!" She laid on the horn and yelled, "Come *on*!"

It took twenty-five minutes to get eastbound on I-40. Felicia asked for the address again, and I gave it to her, on Seventeenth Street, about four blocks north of the Strip on campus.

"Okay, okay," she said, alternating between slamming on the gas and pumping the brake. "I think I know where that it is."

It turned out to be in a row of brownstones converted into student apartments. The entire block had a deserted feel to it, an atmosphere of abandonment, with the leafless oaks and maples and Bradford pears, and the small yards of winter-killed grass.

Felicia parked on the street about half a block to the north.

She cut off the engine and we sat in silence for a few minutes, looking at the house. Someone had wrapped silver tinsel around the porch railing.

"She's had plenty of time to scoot," Felicia said.

"And probably won't come to the door when she sees it's us," I added.

"You're the detective, Ruzak. Now what?"

"Maybe she called him," I said. "Maybe he'll show up."

"Maybe they live together and he has a knife to her throat."

"Maybe we should call the cops."

"Maybe that's the dumbest idea I've ever heard after the way they've screwed this up," she said.

"Well," I said. "If she isn't inside, she's somewhere else. . . ."

"Oh, you're so good."

"And she'll either come back or she won't."

"Right."

"Or she's still inside trying to figure out what to do."

"Calling first was a stupid idea," she said. "I say we stake it out. If she's in, at some point she has to come out. If she's out, odds are at some point she has to go back in."

"Okay," I said.

And so we waited. After about fifteen minutes, Felicia checked in with the sitter, telling her she got tied up at the mall and she might have to stay through dinner. She hung up and looked at me.

"Aren't you going to call Amanda? She might be worried."

"She's at work," I said, avoiding her eyes.

"Maybe you're just in denial, Ruzak. You really are attracted to her, but you're afraid of getting your heart broken."

"Or the opposite," I said. "The last girl broke it and maybe I'm afraid it'll be mended."

The hours drew out, and the snow began to grow fatter, taking longer to melt on the windshield and actually surviving on the exposed tree branches. Every few minutes Felicia started the car to keep us warm. It was nearly three o'clock when she said, "I can see why you're so enamored by this detective deal. Such heart-pounding excitement."

She scrunched down in her seat, pulling the red scarf tighter around her neck. I didn't smell cinnamon now, but peaches with a hint of coconut.

"I'm hungry," she said suddenly.

"There's a Walgreens on the corner," I said. "I'll get us something."

"No. I'll go. You're the big strong man. Did you bring your gun?"

"Why would I bring my gun?"

I watched her walk down the sidewalk toward Cumberland. When I couldn't see her anymore, I watched the house. I looked for any sign of life, any movement in the windows. Nothing.

Felicia came back with some candy bars, a couple of Mountain Dews, and a bag of Bugles.

"Bugles!" I said. "I haven't had those since I was a kid." I tore open the bag and popped a handful into my mouth. Felicia watched me, amused.

"It takes so little, doesn't it, Ruzak?"

The light began to fail. Despite the massive dose of caffeine from my soda, I started to get a little heavy-lidded. I think I dozed off. The next thing I knew, Felicia's head was on my shoulder, her left arm across my body, her hand curled into a fist in my lap, and my world was the smell of coconuts. It was cold inside the car and it was hard to see through the snow-dusted windows, but I didn't wake her. I put my hand over hers, to see if it was cold. I told myself, if her hand was cold I would wake her so she could get the heater going. Her hand didn't seem that cold to me, so I didn't wake her.

Then she stirred—maybe because I touched her—and her arm moved around my waist and she pressed herself closer, moving her head to my chest, and she made some low sound in the back of her throat, a contented purr. I wondered if I was Bob—or a memory of Bob, a kind of Boblike echo—and I had found myself in a situation rooted in a false pretext, the equivalent of a stolen kiss.

Back when I was a security guard and Felicia was a waitress at the Old City Diner, I would make small talk to keep her by my table, because, frankly, there was something about the way her nose crinkled when she laughed. At seven o'clock, my shift had ended; hers had just begun. It was the only hour of the day when our orbits overlapped, and I flattered myself that something might be born in the area formed by the intersection of our spheres.

She wore a white uniform and those thick-soled white shoes over white stockings, her hair always swept back into a tight bun, only a few wisps of blond would hang down in the back, and at the time I wondered how her hair would feel between my fingers. Now that same thick hair was inches beneath my nose, and the smell of coconut made me think of piña coladas, which led to tropical breezes and the rustle of palm trees and the feel of sand beneath your toes, the foam of crashing waves, and the water fading into the sky, even that old Rupert Holmes song, "If you like piña coladas and getting caught in the rain . . ."

I sat very still, skirting along the edge of the moment, maybe the only opportunity I would ever have to touch Felicia's hair. Fifty years from now, would I chase sleep on my deathbed, haunted by my cowardice, my failure of will at the critical hour on that snowy night when she lay curled in my arms? Sometimes we're afforded some space before we must screw our courage to the sticking place, and that's all we need, a little time to steel ourselves. Then there are moments like this one, where the courage must be drawn from some inner reserve before that singular moment is gone forever. With no warning, the test comes, and whatever is beneath the mask you present to the world, the elemental *you,* stripped of pretense, is exposed. Reggie Matthews had one of the moments and, when that moment came, Reggie Matthews ran. In a way, he was still running.

And speaking of runners: Consider Ruzak inside this snow-encrusted car, in the gloaming of an early winter day, as he begins to shiver and not because it's cold. What should I make of him, when even the simplest act forces him to freeze like a tightrope walker teetering on the rope, absurdly paralyzed in midstride, in that instant before the fall?

Really, Ruzak, how much courage does it take to touch a pretty girl's hair?

I raised my hand to touch Felicia's hair.

FORTY-FOUR

*A*nd when I did, she said, "Ruzak, what the hell are you do-ing?"

"Nothing," I said, dropping my hand. She pulled away, touch-ing her hair where I had almost touched it.

"Did I fall asleep?"

"I think we both did."

She pulled down the visor and checked out her face in the mirror.

"Oh God," she said. "I think I drooled."

I looked down at my shirt, but didn't see any evidence of drib-ble.

"Great," she said. "We probably missed her."

I looked down the street. "Maybe, but here comes somebody."

He was wearing a Tennessee orange hoodie and blue jeans, walking toward us from Cumberland Avenue. A short guy, painfully thin, with long dark hair that pooled in the folds of the hood, hands jammed into the hoodie's pocket. He approached us with his head down, so I didn't get a good look at his face. He turned up the walk of the house. The door swung open as he mounted the porch; she must have been watching for him. He disappeared inside.

"Okay," Felicia breathed. "Now what?"

"I don't know," I said. "I thought he'd be bigger."

"You said you didn't get a look at him."

"No. But I had the impression he displaced a lot more air."

"What the hell does *that* mean?"

"You know, like he was more lumbering than lithe. I say we chance it. We might not get another shot at this."

I started to open the door. Felicia grabbed my forearm.

"First tell me what we're chancing, Ruzak."

"We're going to knock on the door."

"We could have done that hours ago."

"We didn't know she was there."

"We still don't know she's there. This guy might not be connected at all. Or maybe her roommate let him in."

"Only one way to find out."

I heaved myself out of the seat. My battered torso sang a little protest song. I leaned against the car, holding my cane, as Felicia got out and met me on the curb. A snowflake clung to her eyelash.

"I'll get to one side," I said. "Between the window and the door. You do the knocking."

"They can see us coming," Felicia murmured as we approached the brownstone.

"He's here now," I said. "I doubt they're hovering by the door, watching."

I leaned on the wall, trying to catch my breath in the thin winter atmosphere. I made a mental note to always carry my gun with me. Then I mentally tore up the note—I'd forgotten I was getting out of the detective business.

I didn't know what I was going to do with my life. Maybe I'd try to get into college and study something that might one day benefit mankind, like medicine. *Dr. Ruzak to the OR, stat!* I watched a lot of the Discovery Health Channel, and the operating room scenes never grossed me out. I wasn't sure how far that went to qualify me to practice medicine, but I wasn't so old yet I had to close that door.

Felicia knocked. We waited. She knocked again.

"'Who's that?'" Felicia whispered. "'Oh, just that beefy detective and his trusty sidekick. Let's let them in!'"

"You could kick down the door using your ninja powers," I suggested.

"And they prosecute us for breaking and entering," she said, which sort of acknowledged that she did have ninja powers.

"They're college students," I said. "I say we go Pavlovian. Yell 'Pizza!'"

"My hands are so cold it hurts to knock."

"What do they want?" I asked rhetorically. "They want us to leave. So we don't. We stay until they realize we won't."

"They've probably already run out the back door."

"You know," I said. "I didn't even consider that."

"You're born for this work, Ruzak, you know that?"

She knocked again, this time an urgent *rap-rap-rap*.

"Somebody's coming," she whispered. "I hear them."

I pressed my back against the wall, in case they were checking her out through the window. I heard the latch turn and the door came open a few inches. I held my breath so the person on the other side wouldn't see it fog.

"Yes?"

"Angela Cummings?" Felicia said.

"Yes?"

"Angela," Felicia said, her tone both kind and urgent. "We know he's here and we want to help. We want to help him and we want to help you help him."

"I don't know what you're talking about," I heard Angela say. "I really don't." But the door stayed open a crack. Felicia should stick her foot between the door and the frame. That was PI 101, but I couldn't expect Felicia to know that.

"We know he's the one," Felicia said. "The police don't, not yet, but close this door and in five minutes they'll have the SWAT team in position."

"He's not. He didn't. They caught the guy who did. He confessed."

"Caught the guy who did what?" Felicia asked. "I thought you didn't know what I was talking about. Look, we're not here to arrest anyone. We just want to talk."

"We?"

I pushed away from the wall and stood behind Felicia. Through the crack, I could see one large, teary eyeball over a slice of nose.

"Hey," the girl said, her voice rising. "I don't know who you people are or who sent you—"

"I'm Teddy Ruzak," I said. "And Jack Minor sent me."

FORTY-FIVE

Behind the girl, a shadow moved, then spoke. "Angela, you better let them in."

The door abruptly swung closed. Felicia looked over her shoulder at me, the red scarf cupping her delicate chin.

"I think she disagrees," she said.

The door opened again, and Angela stepped back to let us pass. Several feet into the gloomy entryway stood the kid in the hoodie. Angela closed the door and threw the deadbolt, and then the four us stood there, and nobody seemed to have anything to say.

"I didn't kill him," the kid said.

"But you were there," I said. "With the guy who did."

He didn't say anything. I went on, "Three of you, and then you mutilated his corpse."

"I didn't," the kid whispered. "I never touched the guy. Eric cut the letters."

"But it was your idea. Angela had told you about the tetra-grammaton. Was that some kind of joke?"

"No." He shook his head. In the weak light spilling from the kitchen behind him, he had all the physical presence of a drug addict. I still couldn't make out his face. "We panicked, man. That other guy, his buddy, he saw us. He saw everything. So Brice took after him, chased him down the street, left us there with the body and we didn't know what to do. So I said, 'Let's make it look like some crazed serial killer did it.' But I didn't do it; I didn't cut him up; it wasn't me. I was saying let's leave a note or something and Eric said we can't leave a note—there'd be fingerprints—and anyway, we didn't have anything to write with, so he found a broken bottle in the alley . . ."

He choked up. Angela brushed past me and stood by his side, pulling his hand into both of hers.

"I said we gotta do this. We gotta do this and in a couple days we'll write a letter to the cops calling ourselves the Yahweh Killers or something like that so they'll think it's some kind of weird cult or something."

"Brilliant plan," Felicia said.

"We were drunk! I mean, shit, I've never been in trouble. I've never even had a fucking traffic ticket! Brice went crazy on the old guy over that hat. That fucking hat!"

"He *is* crazy," Angela said softly. "I told you not to hang out with him."

"Brice was the one who beat me up," I said.

Angela nodded. "I told Liam I was meeting you at the park, and he told Brice."

"You gotta understand," Liam said. "I can't go to prison. Jesus Christ, I'm supposed to graduate this spring!"

"And get married," Angela said softly. "Please, Mr. Ruzak, I've been telling him to go to the cops. They'll go easy on him if he co-operates, right? Won't they cut him a deal if he agrees to testify?"

"I never touched him," Liam cried. "I never touched the old fuck!"

"Stop that," I said. "Don't call him that."

"You shouldn't call him that, Liam," Angela said.

"Where are they? Where are Brice and Eric?" I asked.

"Man, you don't know. Eric isn't so bad, but Brice will fucking *kill* you, man."

I said to Angela, "So after I called you, you called Liam. What about Brice and Eric?"

She shook her head. "I called Liam. Just Liam."

"Did you call them?" I asked Liam. "Do they know that I know?"

"Are you serious? I waited until my shift was up and then I came over here to figure out what to do. I don't know what to do!"

"That's okay," Felicia said. "We do."

FORTY·SIX

*T*hey sat in the backseat on the short drive from campus to downtown, holding hands. Angela urged him into saying the Lord's Prayer with her. I finally got a look at his features: sallow, pinched, pocked by acne scars, and for some reason I thought of Ichabod Crane.

"I'm sorry you got hurt, Mr. Ruzak," Angela offered as we waited for the light to change on the corner of Cumberland and Main. "It's my fault. I saw the flyer on campus and I don't know why I couldn't say anything on the phone. It wasn't about the money. I'm a good person. Liam's a good person. And Eric, he just does whatever Brice tells him to do."

"Eric's a moron," Liam said. "They're both fucking morons."

"I told him not to hang with Brice," Angela said.

"He won't let 'em take him alive," Liam said. "He told me that, if it ever went down."

"What a shame," Felicia said. "I'll miss him."

Liam started to cry. Angela slipped her arm around his shoulder and he collapsed into her chest. She stroked his black, greasy hair and whispered, "It's okay, baby. It's okay. It's going to be okay. Put yourself into the Lord's hands now. Ask Jesus into your heart. Tell him you're sorry and he'll forgive you." I had the feeling I was hearing a reprise of a speech she had given many times. "He loves you, Liam, he loves you so much and you know what? So do I. I don't care what you did. That's what it's about, baby. Love. Love, love, love, baby." She kissed the top of his head. "All things for a reason, baby. All things for a reason."

"Tell that to Jack Minor," Felicia muttered.

"Here's what I don't get," Liam said, his voice coming up muffled between his girlfriend's breasts. "You, Ruzak. I don't get you. Who the hell was that old guy to you? Why the hell do you care?"

"Ruzak is on a mission of God," Felicia said. "His humble instrument."

"Oh, Christ," Liam moaned.

"He's a roundabout operator," I said. "Inscrutable."

The dome of the Sunsphere shone in the night sky behind us; a golden halo shimmered in the falling snow, a circle of beatific light. Why the hell did I care? I didn't answer, because I had come to the point where I understood the question was irrelevant. Only one question really mattered, and it wasn't that one. Maybe

Jack Minor lying dead in my alleyway was the answer, or maybe it was just another way of putting the same question that we've been asking since we dropped from the trees and rose on two legs to survey the landscape: Hello, are you there? Can you hear me? Who are you and what do you want?

The answer eludes us.

DECEMBER 24

FORTY-SEVEN

*B*y midmorning Amanda had packed up, her old duffle by the door with Archie beside it, his dog senses tingling at the impending disintegration of our little pack. I was up by eight, showered and dressed, and made a quick run to the Krispy Kreme while Amanda snored on the sofa. I took Archie with me for a little private time.

"Look," I said, as he stared at me from the passenger seat. "You and I have to come to some sort of understanding here. For better or worse, fate's dumped you into my lap, and we both had better get used to it. I think what gets to me most is this feeling of expectation or dread, the way you just stare at me, like you're afraid I'm going to wig out on you. I'm really a fairly balanced person. I tend to think too much and get too wrapped up in trivialities, sort of a borderline autistic—don't think I haven't thought of that—but that doesn't mean I'm a bad person or, more to the point, a poor owner. I promise to give you a warm place to sleep and tasty kibble and take you on walks and play with you. Well, as long as my super doesn't kick you out—I'm going to have to work on that problem. The point is, I appreciate the fact that you're an excellent listener; it's really impressive the way you seem to cling to my every word, but there's a reason we tell little kids not to stare, you know?"

Amanda was up by the time we returned with the doughnuts. I also picked up a couple of their medium-brew coffees. Like soft-drink products, coffee always tasted better from a restaurant.

"Maybe I should stay," she said. Without her makeup, she looked about twelve years old. "You're going to be alone for Christmas."

"I'm working down at the mission tomorrow," I said. "And you should be home with your family."

"Do you like me, Ruzak?" she asked.

"Sure I like you. I can't thank you enough for helping me through all this."

"You know what I mean."

"I have this difficulty," I said. "This fear of foisting my foibles on others."

"That's stupid," she said. "If everybody waited until they were perfect—"

"Oh, I know I'll never get to that point. I'd just like to be a little more sure of what I want."

"The plain truth is you don't find me attractive. Why can't you say that? And if you're afraid you'll hurt my feelings, tell me what's worse: finding me unattractive and lying about it or thinking I'm gross and telling me the truth?"

"That's sort of a false choice."

"So you do find me attractive, and this is all about you not knowing what you want?"

"Well."

"Ruzak, how can you decide what you want unless you try it? It's like deciding you don't like sushi without ever tasting it."

She licked the glaze from her fingertips. Before I allowed myself to think, I leaned forward and kissed her sugary lips. Our eyes met for an instant, and then she slapped me very hard across the left cheek.

"Bastard," she said.

I offered to walk her to her car. She told me she was perfectly capable of walking by herself.

"I'll call you," I said.

"Don't."

She wasn't gone five minutes when the phone rang. I was so sure it was her, I didn't bother to look at the caller ID.

"Hello, Mr. Ruzak," Detective Black said. "Just wanted to let you know we got Brice Carlson last night."

"Alive?"

"Surrendered without incident. He was holed up at his parents' house down in Polk County. Denies everything, but Eric Reston broke yesterday and confessed."

"It's done," I said.

"All but the shouting."

"Well," I said. "Thanks for letting me know."

"We'd like to go after him for the assault on you," she said. "We've got Angela's and Liam's testimony and we can get Brice's cell phone records—Liam stated he called him that afternoon."

"I don't think so," I said.

"Excuse me?"

"I don't think so. You've got him on Jack. That's enough."

"You're sure?"

I told her I was, down to my shoestrings.

"Okay. I had one more thing."

"What's that?"

"An apology. You were right and I was wrong. You know," she said. "In six years as a homicide detective, I've never encountered a case quite like this one. I've never had an eyewitness confess to something he didn't do. I just wanted you to understand there was no bad faith involved. We honestly thought we had the right guy."

It was more of an acknowledgment than an apology, but I didn't press it.

"And if you hadn't stuck to your guns, an innocent man might have paid a very dear price."

"Right," I said. "One's enough."

"One's enough?"

"I mean Jack. Don't get me wrong, detective, I'm glad we got these boys, but it's one of those things that bring closure but no satisfaction."

"I don't understand what you mean, Mr. Ruzak."

"Three college kids on a drunk kill a harmless homeless person over a hat. My understanding is this Brice character was nothing but a punk and a thug, but these other two weren't bad kids, just weak, and now they have no future, and Jack is dead, though I guess you could say he didn't have a future, either. It just seems so . . . useless."

"Sounds to me like somebody's got the Christmas blues."

"Oh, I'm an optimist at heart," I said. "But if you're gonna get in the water, you gotta risk a riptide or two."

A day after his father's release from prison, Robert Matthews showed up at my door with his dad in hand and a chip on his shoulder.

"I oughta punch you in the face for what you did to my old man," Robert said.

"Ruzak didn't do anything to me," Reggie said.

"Did I ask for your input?" Robert asked him. "Look, Ruzak, we had a deal and I'm not leavin' town without the balance of what you owe me."

"What I owe Reggie, you mean."

"Whatever!"

"The reward was, I think, um, rewardable upon arrest and *conviction . . .*"

"That's not what you told me in Johnson City."

"But if you read the flyer—"

"You told me one half right now and the next half when some-body went to jail. Well, I read the papers. Somebody's in jail—where's my twelve-fifty?"

"*My* twelve-fifty," Reggie said.

"Whatever! Plus the fact I should sue you for breach of con-tract, Ruzak, kidnapping under false pretenses; I don't know, I'm not a fucking lawyer, but they threw my dad in prison after beat-ing a false confession out of him, and you didn't even bother to tell me!"

"They didn't beat me," Reggie said. "I confessed falsely of my own free will."

"In fact," Robert said, jabbing his finger at my nose, "you lied about it! You told me he was living here!"

"He asked me not to tell you."

"Why?"

"Maybe that's a question you should ask him."

"Look, I didn't come all this way to bandy words with you, dickhead."

"Bandy?"

"I just want what's mine."

"Mine," Reggie said.

"Whatever!"

"Let me get my checkbook," I said.

So I wrote out a check to Reggie Matthews for $12,500. Then I handed the check to Reggie. I wished them both a Merry Christmas and a Happy New Year. I closed the door and heard Robert saying loudly in the hall, "Dad, if I let you keep it, it'll be gone in a month!"

I felt bad for Reggie, but told myself that whole setup was an accident of nature, which really had nothing to do with me.

After getting off the phone with Detective Black, I took Archie for a walk, wrapping him in my overcoat for the trip outside lest Whittaker or one of his spies was on the prowl. Then I went back upstairs, where I put on a pot of coffee because I still had half a dozen Krispy Kremes left and nobody to share them with. Archie sat at my feet and stared while I chewed.

"Not good for you," I said. "And besides, nobody likes a beggar."

And of course I thought of Jack when I said it, and not how I usually thought of him, tossed on a pile of garbage, dead eyes wide open, but the day before, standing by my car in the middle of the street, the questioning look when I passed my hat through the open window. *God bless,* he murmured. The way he appeared in my rearview mirror as I drove away, clutching that hat, astounded by his good fortune, a solitary figure standing on a street corner in the rain, as ubiquitous and forgettable as any street person.

Beggars can't be choosers. If wishes were horses, a beggar could ride. My mother had a boatload of sayings, a seemingly endless supply of bromides for every possible occasion, I guess because clichés are the convenient hooks we use for hanging our hats of uncertainty.

I washed up in the kitchen sink, scrubbing my hands until the knuckles turned raw. Something felt like it was slipping inside, so acting on instinct—maybe the same instinct that drove me to give Jack my floppy hat—I put Archie in his cage and headed downstairs for my car.

I stopped at Walgreens first and purchased a stocking with an embroidered puppy on the front, filled with bones and chewies and a little packet of breath fresheners, sort of like Tic Tacs for canines.

A year ago on this night, I was at Mom's house leafing through old photos of Christmases past. There's Dad pulling another shirt from a box. There's Teddy with his first bike. There's your cousin Ernie from New Jersey, don't you remember him? I wondered what happened to those albums—did I stick them in my closet? Our old house in Fountain City had a big fireplace where Mom hung our stockings, three in a row, until Dad died, and then there were two. Where did those end up? I tried to remember if I had a box in the closet labeled "Christmas." If I found mine and put it out tonight, how much faith did I have it would be filled to overflowing on Christmas morning?

I pulled into the Park Rite lot beside the Ely Building and Lonny came out of his little booth, a cigarette dangling from his mouth.

"Saw they caught the bastards," he said.

I nodded. "They did."

He trailed behind me as I trudged up the walk toward the entrance.

"You oughta take a look at the alley."

"Why?"

"They cleaned it up. Put up some little tables. Looks like the outside of a little French bistro back there now."

"That'll be nice when the weather warms up."

He hovered beside me at the door. I wasn't sure what he wanted.

"You don't have to work on Christmas, do you?" I asked.

He shook his head. "Naw. Gotta scramble tonight, though— still don't have all my shopping done."

"Me either."

I went upstairs, past the dry cleaners, three flights up to my door, where someone had posted a sticky note on the frosted glass: *Mr. Ruzak please call me. I need your help.* I didn't recognize the name. There was a small pile of mail on the floor below the slot. I scooped it up and dropped it on Felicia's desk. It was cold inside; my breath fogged around my head as I went into my office. A fine patina of dust covered the desk, the globe in the corner, the bookcase with the full leather-bound set of the *Tennessee Rules of Evidence* that Felicia had mail-ordered to give my shelves some gravitas.

The blinds were drawn. Funny, I couldn't remember doing that. I pulled the thin cord to open them and stared out the window to the alley three stories below. The glass fogged with the impression of my breath, evidence of my autonomy: take that, Eunice Shriver!

In an instant, scientists tell us (in theory born in the mind of a priest), the universe spontaneously burst into existence, spewing out the matter that would form you and me a few billion years later, after violent cataclysms, stars and proto-planets smashing into each other, after mass extinctions and millions of years of evolution, the arrival of Teddy Ruzak in this moment, slouching in his rumpled overcoat, scrubbing his three-day-old beard with the back of his hand, standing before a foggy window slightly pigeon-toed, with a crooked nose and a bent walk, a triumph of Nature's inscrutable design, the current occupant in this empty space, at once obscure and of paramount import.

It was like I told Angela: I knew the *who,* the *what,* and the *where*. It was the *why,* the motive. Someone once said we were here because the universe needed a way to look at itself. We were Creation's eyes.

I closed the blinds and turned from the window. I knew these rooms like the back of my hand, but that didn't change the fact that I was still in the dark.

I had solved the case but not the mystery.

FORTY-EIGHT

I stopped at the Barnes & Noble, then doubled back to Middlebrook Pike. The home was maybe five miles from the bookstore, and it took me forty-five minutes to get there, the traffic was so bad.

The receptionist at the desk took my name and told me to have a seat, and another ten minutes crawled by. Here's Ruzak again, putting in his time, filling his quota. Finally, an attendant wearing hospital-type gear, including the soft-soled shoes and scrublike top, escorted me to a room they called the Solarium. The lighting was weak and washed out, a feeble, whispery-thin light; maybe the room was more solariumish in the summers.

Eunice Shriver was sitting in a rocking chair by a door marked FOR HOSPICE PERSONNEL ONLY. All the window seats were taken.

I didn't recognize her at first. She'd always been meticulous about her makeup, and now I saw her for the first time without it. They had taken her wig away, too, and her natural hair was thin and wispy. I could see her irregularly shaped, bone-white scalp. She was wearing a purple terrycloth robe and matching slippers.

"Well," she said as I pulled up a chair. "Look what the cat drug in."

"Merry Christmas, Eunice," I said. I pulled the Barnes & Noble bag out of my coat pocket.

"What's that?"

"It's for you. Sorry, I didn't have it wrapped."

She peeked into the bag, pursing her lips.

"It's a journal," I said. "And also a pen. See, the cap has an *S* on it."

"Why an *S*?"

"*S* for your name."

"My name is Eunice."

"I know. The *S* is for *Shriver*. They didn't have an *E* pen. I looked."

"Well. Thank you, Theodore." She laid the bag on her lap.

"I didn't know if they allowed you to have your computer or typewriter or whatever it is you use to write, so I thought you could use this journal."

"Yes, so you did."

"What, you don't want to write anymore?"

"Oh, I finished the book."

"You did?"

"And I have several publishers interested in it."

"You're kidding."

"I most certainly am not kidding. I shall use a pen name, of course."

"Why?"

"Did Poe use his real name? Did Conan Doyle?"

"Actually, I think they did."

"I picked the name of a local author, though this person's quite obscure, something just shy of a hack, so I'm certain they won't mind."

"What's her name? So I know where to look in the bookstore."

She told me. I said, "Eunice, that's a man's name."

"Ever hear of George Eliot?"

"No."

"Well, there you have it."

"Did you change my name too?"

"Dear heavens, why would I do that?"

"So I wouldn't sue you for libel."

She laughed. Even her eyes seemed washed out in this room of dying light. Ah, Christ, Eunice! Ah, Christ, light! I was gripping the arms of my chair, hard. Something was definitely stuck in my craw. But every time I tried to trap it or tamp it down, it skittered away.

Across the room, beside the upright piano against the wall, a five-foot Christmas tree stood, wrapped in gold tinsel and festooned with red and silver balls. An angel sat on the top, listing to one side so she appeared to be cocking her head toward the ground while she strummed her harp, trying to keep time with an earthly rhythm section. It occurred to me that any attempt to straddle the divide was doomed to failure. The distance between faith and reason was widening, and the time had come to pick sides.

"Eunice," I said. "Do you ever get scared?"

"Why should I be scared?"

"I mean, you must think about it. You know it can't be much longer. Do you think once it's done, it's done and there's nothing afterward? Like those crash tests when the car hits the wall. I guess that's it. Is it a wall or is it an open door, or like a—like some kind of—I don't know, like a porous membrane, opaque but—but through it we shall pass? Because here's the problem as I see it: If it is a wall, then you'll never know you were wrong."

"I would prefer not to," she said.

"But what I'm asking . . . what I'm trying to get at . . . Eunice, are you ever afraid? It won't be long before you'll either meet oblivion or its utter opposite. I'm sure you've thought about it."

"I do not worry about what's next, Theodore. I worry about what's left."

"So 'What's next?' is a pointless question because it can't be answered?"

"Well, that hasn't stopped people from trying to answer it, has it?"

"That's the rub, I guess. In my line of work, you gotta go where the evidence leads you. Take something along the lines of three drunk college kids murdering a mentally incompetent homeless man. What's that evidence of? We all have a destiny, and Jack's is to be beaten to death and dumped on a pile of garbage? Or Jack is being punished for some grand transgression, either in this life or another? Or God gave these boys free will so they could murder a harmless old man just for the hell of it, just because they could? Don't all these possibilities point away from an all-knowing, all-loving, all-powerful Presence and toward that wall, and we're the dummies behind the wheel?"

She stared at me for a long moment.

"Oh, Theodore," she said. "You're so marvelously inept, so hopelessly lost. How I love you."

She placed a withered hand over mine and gave it a squeeze.

"Here's what it is," she said, squeezing. "Here's what it is," squeezing, "and I am so happy, so very grateful that you are mine." Squeezing.